CARNATIONS AND CHAOS

PORT DANBY COZY MYSTERY #2

LONDON LOVETT

CHAPTER 1

louds had hung low in the sky every morning for the past week, but this morning a crisp blue sky showed up to coax me out of bed. But my limbs and back hadn't been quite as eager to exit my downy blanket cocoon. I'd stayed late at the shop, well past dark, to finish the floral arrangements for the Third Annual Food Fair to be held in Port Danby's town square. It had taken one interminably long shower, a cup of coffee and one of Elsie's blueberry muffins to get me out the door and onto my bicycle.

It felt as if I'd just left the shop as I pedaled along Harbor Lane. My pet crow, Kingston, had flown on ahead of me. I could see his shiny black silhouette as he perched on the edge of the shop roof. The flowering plums that lined Harbor Lane were almost completely devoid of foliage, so Kingston had no place to perch and scare songbirds and pretend to be a real crow.

Oddly enough, an unusually long line of customers seemed to be snaked along the sidewalk in front of Elsie's Sugar and Spice Bakery. The tail end of the line was in front of my shop. I got off my bicycle and maneuvered my way through the people. I hadn't noticed that my friend, Lola, was standing amongst the other customers until she called my name.

"Pink, you're here early. Join me." She was near the end of the line. I leaned my bike against the flower shop door and walked over to her.

"What are you doing? Is this all for the bakery?"

"I would have thought you'd already guessed it with your super nose." I wondered how long it would be before the people of Port Danby would stop referring to my nose as super. I had a heightened sense of smell, but it was hardly super. Well, maybe a little super.

"Elsie made some of her famous cinnamon rolls. She only makes them a few times a year because she says they just take too much work and time and space in her ovens. And if you sit at one of her tables to eat one of her magical cinnamon rolls, you get it for free. Which is why there's such a long line. Everyone is waiting for the tables to empty so they can sit and eat."

"I can't decide if that's a genius or ridiculous marketing scheme. I'm going with the latter because after all that work and the expense, Elsie isn't going to make any profit." I looked along the line of anxiously waiting cinnamon roll eaters. "In fact, I'd say she is going to be in the red on this one."

I glanced over to the Coffee Hutch. Elsie's brother, Lester, had almost no customers, and his tables were empty. Unfortunately, I had been the catalyst for The Great Port Danby Table War. My flower shop, Pink's Flowers, had once been Elsie's bakery. She had moved next door because it was a bigger building for her very successful bakery. Now my shop sat between the bakery and the coffee shop, each with its own set of tables and chairs. A healthy dose of sibling rivalry, that apparently never faded with time, not even when the siblings, twins in this case, were well into their sixties, had both shop owners competing to fill their storefront tables. It was usually sort of amusing, but today, it was impacting the entire sidewalk. And poor Lester's mood. Lester stared out the front window of his shop, looking a little droopy. Even though I'd had a cup of coffee at home, I decided to walk over and buy one from lonely Lester.

I unlocked my shop door to push my bicycle inside. Behind me there was a short gasp from the people in line. I ducked and felt the breeze from Kingston's wings as he flew inside to his window perch.

I couldn't hold back a smile when I saw the colorful flower arrangements I'd created for the food fair booths. What better way to pay homage to autumn than with a small bouquet of red, orange, yellow and lavender carnations. I'd placed each colorful bundle into a sleek, slim necked vase and tied dark purple ribbon and orange paper raffia around each one. I hoped that Yolanda Petri, the councilwoman in charge of the fair, would be pleased.

"I'll be right back, Kingston," I said and then silently asked myself why I always felt the need to let my bird know my plans. I let my cat, Nevermore, know too. As if he cared. As long as I wasn't taking the couch or his bowl of food with me, he never even blinked a cat eyelash at seeing me walk out the door.

I circled around to the Coffee Hutch with its sadly empty tables and chairs. The shop itself could hardly be described as sad though. The Coffee Hutch matched its name perfectly, neat and to the point. It was an understated little shop with one flashy concession, a long awning with coffee brown stripes. The brown and white trim on the front window matched the colors of the awning. The front door, which was mostly wavy glass, was trimmed in the same brown. Even the sign above the door was painted in brown and white. With the rich smell of freshly brewed coffee consistently drifting through the windows and door, there really wasn't a need for flashy decor out front. The perpetual aroma was its own pleasant, comforting form of advertisement.

Lester was behind the counter stacking paper cups when I walked inside. The interior of the Coffee Hutch was tiny, but Lester used every inch of space available. Aside from the three tables out front, two long picnic style tables, complete with benches and scarred surfaces, took up the center of the space. But the heart and brains of the shop were tucked, layered and stored neatly behind the shiny black order counter. Two metal pendant lights hung over the coffee brewing station giving the place an appropriately industrial vibe.

"Morning, Les."

"Hey, Lacey. How has your morning been? Better than mine, I hope." A retired fireman and widower, I had hoped that Lester would eventually come to his senses and realize that there were far more important things in life than having more customers at his tables than his sister. But those hopes were dashed when the man, a highly sensible person in every other respect, invested in expensive uphol-stered chair cushions for his outdoor chairs. Unfortunately, in his quest for elegance and plushy comfort, he'd forgotten to buy weather proof cushions. So the brightly colored floral cushions (a conscious choice by a man whose everyday apparel included a Hawaiian shirt, no matter what the weather) had to be brought in every evening and then carried out the next day.

"I'll have a mocha latte with extra whipped cream." I decided a little indulgence would help get me through a long morning with the ener-getic, effervescent Yolanda Petri.

"I'll mix that right up for you." Lester turned to his barista work station. "How come you're not in that long line for the cinnamon rolls? I hear they're free. As long as you sit at the tables," he added with a grumble that I was sure was only meant for his own ears.

"From the looks of it, Elsie is not going to make much profit today. Everyone's waiting for a table."

He spun around looking a little more cheery than when I'd walked inside. "That's what I told the silly woman, but she's more interested in getting those tables filled. It's ridiculous."

I cleared my throat. "Said the man who spent the first fifteen minutes of his work day tying expensive cushions to his outdoor chairs."

A sheepish grin crossed his face beneath his cloud of snow white hair. "I suppose it is getting a little out of hand."

"A little."

Lester handed me the mocha latte. I'd just taken the first sip when Yolanda came briskly into the coffee shop. "There you are, Lacey." She took a deep, steadying breath as if she'd climbed to the top of Everest and back looking for me. "Are the arrangements ready? The men are setting up the booths."

Yolanda Petri lived one street over from me on Shire Lane. She was a forty something with two daughters, Olivia and Tricia, both in middle school. Her husband ran a tire shop in Mayfield, and Yolanda worked as a part-time teacher's aide. In between work and family, she was an active member of the Port Danby City Council. And this year, because she didn't already have enough on her full plate, she had taken charge of the Third Annual Food Fair, an eclectic gathering of all the top food bloggers.

Yolanda was proud (and rightfully so) that she'd convinced the food fair coordinators to let Port Danby host the event. Naturally, she wanted everything to be perfect. Today she looked a little frazzled, but she was still well put together with a blazer, nice jeans and a colorful scarf. She had a cute bobbed haircut and she loved to wear bright orange lipstick, a color that only looked good on a few people. Yolanda happened to be one of those people.

I paid Lester for the coffee, and Yolanda and I walked back over to the flower shop.

"What's happening at Elsie's?" she asked as we skirted through the line.

"Free cinnamon rolls." I opened the door and waved her inside.

Yolanda stopped in front of the line of carnation filled vases. She put her hands on her hips.

I fretted for a moment, thinking she was disappointed. "Will these do?" I asked tentatively.

My flower shop and my status as a Port Danby local were still new, and I found myself still wanting to make a good impression on everyone. With the exception of Mayor Price, who had taken an early disliking to me. I'd decided not to worry about it.

"Lacey 'Pink' Pinkerton," she said sternly and then turned with a wide smile. "I love them!"

CHAPTER 2

*A*fter loading the flower vases into the trunk of Yolanda's car, I spent the rest of the morning working on my Thanksgiving centerpieces. I'd decided to make three examples for customers to choose from, and I was quite pleased with the way they were turning out. I certainly hadn't thought ahead when I decided to open a flower shop just weeks before the long holiday season. For the most part, it had turned out to be a bonus. Flowers were a big deal during the holidays, giving my business a nice start. Enough so, that I'd made the executive decision, me being the sole executive, to hire some help before December.

The goat bell on the front door woke Kingston from his nap. He immediately began a show off dance along his perch when he saw his second favorite human, Lola, walk inside. Lola owned the antique shop across the street. She was my closest friend in Port Danby.

"I need sustenance," she huffed as she hopped up on the stool at my work table. "I've been unpacking the boxes my parents sent from Turkey. Some cool stuff. Some weird and musty smelling stuff too. Now I'm starved."

"Didn't you just eat one of Elsie's cinnamon rolls?"

"Like two hours ago, and by the time I got up to the counter to order one, all she had left were the small end pieces. Poor Elsie, I don't know what she was thinking giving all those rolls away for free. She made no money and customers lingered around her shop all morning just to sit at the tables. Elsie and Lester need to stop this table battle."

"I couldn't agree more." I finished cleaning up the dried moss and splinters of stems littered across my work table. "Maybe we should ask Elsie to come with us to Franki's diner. She could probably use a break."

Lola dropped her feet down to the floor. She was wearing a long sleeved t-shirt with a skull and crossbones on the front. She usually wore funky shirts with her faded jeans, but this one was particularly unique.

"You're looking a little pirate like today, Lola. If you need a fake parrot for your shoulder, I happen to have a bird that would be more than happy to sit on your shoulder all day."

"King-King, my love, the only guy who pays me any attention," Lola crooned as she headed to the bird's perch.

Kingston shuffled back and forth and bobbed his black head up and down until Lola rubbed it. I walked to the sink to wash my hands while she talked to Kingston.

The bell clanged and Elsie shuffled in as if she were dragging heavy weights behind her. Elsie was the fittest person I knew, a disciplined runner who never overindulged in her own pastries. "What a morning. I no longer care about my tables. Lester can have all the customers on his side. I surrender."

Lola and I exchanged secret glances because we both knew that it was just talk, especially because Elsie made the same declaration of surrender at least once a week.

"Lola and I were just heading over to Franki's for lunch. Why don't you join us? I've got to fortify myself before heading over to the town square to help Yolanda set up."

"Lunch sounds good. I'll just go lock up the bakery."

Lola gave Kingston some bird seed and peanuts, and we headed over to the bakery. The table area looked as if it had been hit by a hurricane that had been dropping napkins and paper plates instead of rain. Even the inside of the bakery looked less pristine than usual.

With the exception of the trail of napkins and sticky crumbs on the counter, it was still my favorite shop interior. The perfectly wonderful teal color on the front of the bakery flowed seamlessly inside where it trimmed the country style wood panels running along the massive curved glass counter. Silver trays and pearly white tiered plates proudly presented Elsie's incredible sugar glazed treats. In perfectly quaint contrast to the glossy teal paint, the entire rear wall of the bakery was covered with weathered bricks. A long steel table was set up along the bricks to give Elsie a place to stand in her peach and green checkered apron and fill orders into taffy pink pastry boxes. And that was to say nothing about the conglomeration of mouth watering aromas floating through the air like strands of cotton candy in a floss machine.

Elsie came out from the back room with her purse, and the three of us headed out to the sidewalk for the brief journey to Franki's Diner. As we walked, several trucks rolled along Harbor Lane, heading toward Pickford Way and the town square.

"That must be some of the bloggers," I said. "I know a few had asked if they could come early to set up."

"I think this is going to cause a lot of chaos in town," Elsie said grumpily, an unusual mood for her.

"I think you're just tired from this morning," Lola noted. "You'll see it less as chaos and better for business once you rest."

Elsie shot Lola a disapproving scowl. "Maybe better business for you, but then the fair isn't going to be filled with antique booths."

I glanced over at Lola. "Elsie has a point. Of course, I'm sure none of the goodies at the fair will compare to the treasures inside your bakery."

Elsie who was usually easily flattered wasn't having any of it today. She was obviously over tired and, most likely, disappointed that she'd decided to give away so many cinnamon rolls. Maybe today's fiasco really would be the end of the table war.

"I'm thinking about ordering some heating lamps for my outside eating area," Elsie commented as we walked inside the diner.

Or maybe not.

"That was history's shortest surrender," Lola muttered into my ear as we looked for a table.

Franki had several servers on the floor, but she made a point to come over and say hello. "You three look exhausted, and the fair hasn't even started yet. I'm not sure if I should expect a big rush or a really slow weekend, considering there will be so much food to sample at the event. To be honest, I'm hoping for the slow weekend. I could use it."

"That's a good way to look at it," Elsie said with a decisive nod. She perked up after Franki's pep talk. "I'll have the roast beef dip, extra onions."

"Ooh, I'll have the same," Lola said. "Hold the onions though."

I browsed the menu once more. "I need something that'll give me energy to keep up with Yolanda and that won't make me want to curl up under a tree for a nap." I ran my finger down the menu. "Got it. Soup and salad combo, please."

Franki collected the menus. "Kimi and Kylie are excited because they were hired to work up at the Hawksworth Mansion this weekend. You know how those out-of-towners love to immerse themselves in the sordid, haunted history of that old place. My girls will be there selling five dollar tickets to see the collection inside the gardener's shed."

The Hawksworth Manor, a decaying gothic mansion that sat perched on Maple Hill behind my house, had been the site of a grisly murder, the entire Hawksworth family wiped out, just after the turn of the last century. The police at the time had closed the case as a murder-suicide deciding that jealousy had driven Bertram Hawksworth to kill his entire family before taking his own life. Since murder mysteries had always intrigued me, I was determined to find out more about the century old tragedy. But aside from an embarrassing and frightening mishap, where I found myself locked inside the mansion's dark entry, I hadn't done much research yet. Now with the gardener's shed and all its grim displays and pictures open for viewing, I might have found my chance. I'd have to make time to visit.

"I'll bet the girls are excited, Franki," I said.

Franki was a business owner and single mother to four teenagers. She was amazing.

"Oh yes. They will each make a hundred dollars. I can tell you those two have already been scouring the internet for things to buy with that money. I suggested something practical like school supplies or new winter coats and they nearly laughed me out of their bedroom." She straightened the menus in her hand. "I'll get this order in."

Elsie seemed to have revived some. She sat back with her glass of ice water. "I know several of the food bloggers coming in for the fair. I went to pastry school with a couple of them. One of them, Marian Fitch, is quite famous and wealthy now." Elsie crinkled her nose. "A most undeserving woman at that. She was terribly unlikable. But she has a bestselling cookbook. Although, knowing Marian, she probably stole most of the recipes."

Lola sat forward. "Enough about Marian." Her brown eyes twinkled as she looked across the table at me. "The big question is—who are you going to dance with first tomorrow night, Pink? Dash or Detective Briggs?" Yolanda had decided to kick off the weekend fair with a big dance.

My cheeks warmed. I hadn't expected the question nor had I given the dance or my prospective partners much thought. "First, who said I was planning to dance? And secondly, if Detective James Briggs shows up to the dance, I will eat my hat."

Lola patted down her own straw hat, one of many hats she wore to tame down her curly red hair. "You don't wear a hat, so you'll have to eat mine."

"Seriously, I've hardly talked to Detective Briggs since I helped him solve Beverly Kent's murder. He's a busy man, and he is the least likely person I expect to see at the dance. I'm sure Dash will be there, but then, I'm also sure his 'dance card' is probably already full. Which is absolutely fine."

Lola shook her head. "That's a terrible attitude. It's a dance, my friend, and I expect to see you out on the dance floor strutting your stuff and doing embarrassing dance moves just like the rest of us."

I laughed. "We'll see."

CHAPTER 3

*T*he southwest corner of Port Danby, where the Pickford Lighthouse stood watch over the steep, granite and shale cliffs, was a lovely choice for the food fair. The town square afforded a picturesque view of the wilderness that lay just beyond the city offices. The tiny brick house that was the mayor's office and the neighboring, uninspiring buildings next to it had a stunning backdrop of various tall trees, each lush with crisp autumn foliage. The leaves of towering ash trees fluttered in the coastal breeze like a swarm of boysenberry and blush pink butterflies. Several majestic red maples stretched their thinning branches, filling the sky with pops of crimson red. The delicate, frilly leaves of the katsura trees framed the gray shingles of the roof tops with a smear of honey yellow. And farther in, ironwood trees surrounded the town square like obedient sentries, boasting wide leaves that reminded me of a glowing orange sunset.

"I love fall, don't you?" I asked Yolanda as I handed her two more carnation vases. She barely took the time to respond.

Yolanda had a good ten years plus on me, but the spry woman was running circles around me as we helped deliver flowers and balloons to each of the booths. Plain, utilitarian style booths with white canopies had been set up along the entire border of the town square. The flowers and balloons would add some nice color, but the real color would come once the bloggers hung banners and piled luscious treats for display and sampling. Several of the bloggers had arrived early and were already decorating their booths.

One woman, who looked a few years older than me, was hanging a long banner with the blog name, 'Down Home Comfy' emblazoned in bright blue along a pink gingham checked background. She seemed a little nervous or excited or maybe both. Or maybe it was just the extremely large cup of coffee sitting on the corner of her booth next to the massive bottle of cooking oil. She had thin red hair, that she made seem even thinner by wearing it long and combed down the middle. I noticed a long string of whimsical butterflies tattooed along the inside of her arm as I handed her a cluster of balloons.

"Hello, I'm your resident balloon and flower distributor, Lacey Pinkerton. I own the flower shop in town." I shook her hand.

"Twyla Walton of Down Home Comfy. Which I guess is obvious because of the banner." Her fingers shook a bit as she stuck her hair behind her ears. "Sorry, I'm a little overwhelmed. This is my first fair."

"Mine too." I pointed at the balloons. "Of course, I'm just handing out decorations. I'm sure you'll do fine." I leaned back and read the small print on the banner. "First, let me say, I love your logo. You can't go wrong with a quirky drawing of a cross-eyed sheep. I will have to visit your blog. I see you specialize in southern comfort food. I'm a big fan of food that gives comfort."

She smiled, but it was weak, a bit forced. She really was uneasy. "I'm sort of new to southern cooking. I used to be a pastry chef but that's over." Twyla waved her hand, giving short flight to her ink butterflies, before fidgeting with her hair again. "Anyhow, that's not important. Thank you so much for the balloons."

"I'll let you get back to setting up. If you need anything, just yell." As I turned to walk away, a deep voice rained down on me from above.

"O.K. I need help."

I spun around and shaded my eyes to keep down the glare from the blue sky. But even with the blinding sunlight, it was easy to see Dash's wide smile.

"How could I possibly have missed my six foot plus neighbor standing on a ladder?"

"You forgot incredibly handsome." Dash pointed to the tool box on the ground. Yolanda had him stringing garlands of lights around and across the town square. "Could you bring me the wire cutters from that box? They look like angry edged pliers."

I put my hands on my hips. "Excuse me, but I *am* a florist. I think I can pick out a pair of wire cutters."

Dash laughed. "What was I thinking?"

I rummaged through the tools and found the wire cutters. I walked to the bottom of the ten to twelve foot ladder and stared up at the bottom of Dash's work boots. "I have the pliers."

"Great. Just climb up a few rungs, and I should be able to reach them. If I let this strand go, it'll fall and get tangled. And I've spent more than enough time untangling these lights."

"You asked for the wire cutters, but you didn't mention that it required climbing." I held the wire cutters as well as I could as I took hold of the ladder with both hands. "Will it hold us both?"

"Sure. Just climb steadily. The entire thing is balancing against a light pole."

I managed to get three rungs up without causing any catastrophe. "This is it. I'm at my climbing adventure limit." Clinging to the ladder with my free hand, I stretched my arm up. The ladder wobbled a bit as Dash leaned down and snatched it from my fingers.

Precarious as our balancing act seemed, he took the time to flash me a flirtatious smile. "First dance tomorrow night?"

"Me? I suppose. But I have to warn you, I don't dance much better than I climb ladders."

"Then you're in luck because I am a fine dancer. I think it's in the Vanhouten blood."

I laughed and climbed back down. "Right, what with all those elaborate balls and glitzy parties you Vanhoutens have to attend."

Dash's real name, Dashwood Vanhouten the third had been fabricated by his father, a salesman, who wanted people to think he came from a rich, important family. The man was clearly brilliant.

"Yoo hoo, Lacey," Yolanda called across the square. She was holding another cluster of balloons. I headed over to her and took hold of the balloons.

Two very young looking bloggers, a man and a woman, were hanging a banner that had the letters DAB printed across it. The small print said *vegan recipes for people who love adventure and our furry friends.*

"Here are some balloons to decorate your booth. I'm Lacey, if you need anything."

"Hey, how's it going? Byron, and this is my girlfriend, Daisy." Byron was a little shorter than me, (and I wasn't tall) with a long red beard, a purple knit beanie and an oversized shirt. Daisy had a felt bowler pressed down over her short dark hair, and one ear had at least a dozen tiny gold hoops running along the lobe.

Byron tied a balloon to the pole holding up the canopy. "Actually, do you know where we can buy some wheat grass for our power smoothies? Daisy forgot to pack the wheat grass."

"The wheat grass was your responsibility," Daisy chirped from the back of the booth where she was busy pulling ingredients out of linen shopping bags.

"I can't think of any shop in Port Danby that has it, but I know there's a health food store in Mayfield, which is the town just east of here."

"Oh right. That's where we're staying. In the Mayfield Hotel," Byron said.

I was surprised. I took them as more of the toss up a tent on the beach type of duo but then what did I know. "So some of the bloggers are staying in Mayfield? I just assumed everyone was staying here at the Port Danby Motel. But thinking about it, that makes sense. There aren't that many rooms in the motel."

"Yeah, we saw a few of the fair participants pulling into the hotel parking lot as we left. Daisy and I wanted to get a head start. We've got lots of fruits and vegetables to cut."

"Well, I will let you get back to work. Just let me know if you need anything."

"Yoo hoo, Lacey!" Yolanda called, yet again, from across the square. At this rate, I might just be too tired for the dance.

CHAPTER 4

*E*lsie, who I'd quickly discovered was never one to stay grumpy or melancholy for long, had come up with a brilliant plan during her Wednesday evening run. She'd surmised that the one treat that would not be served at the fair were Port Danby Icon Cookies. Of course, those did not exist until her brilliantly clever mind came up with them. Each massive sugar cookie would have a fondant decoration of one of three Port Danby landmarks, the Pickford Lighthouse, Graystone Church and she'd even created a tiny fondant Hawksworth Mansion (imagined in its former glory, of course).

The only flaw in her new plan was that she had very little time to prepare the cookies and have them ready to sell when the fair attendees started flowing into town. This meant a three o'clock in the morning cookie assembly line. I had volunteered to help her, and Lola begrudgingly signed on too, even though she claimed she didn't know how to walk, talk or function at that hour.

The bakery was already filled with the buttery sweet aroma of the cookies by the time Lola and I dragged ourselves in at three. Lola sat immediately down on one of Elsie's stools, holding her coffee as if her life depended on it. In the meantime, Elsie and I organized a production line. The tiny, fit woman of boundless energy had been up all night cutting out tiny sugar and fondant decorations for the cookies.

The tiny white, black and red lighthouse was my favorite. But then I was a big fan of the Pickford Lighthouse. It was one of the things that had drawn me to Port Danby.

Elsie had used a grayish purple fondant for the silhouette of the gothic mansion. She'd even managed to get the turrets and gable pitch on the roof just right. The Graystone Church had tiny yellow and blue fondant squares in the windows for stained glass.

"My gosh, Elsie, you are a genius. These look amazing. I think they'll be the perfect Port Danby souvenir, and I'm sure they'll taste way better than anything served at the fair. And, yes, this extreme flattery is my subtle way of asking for a cookie sample."

Elsie nodded. "I saved all the broken pieces figuring you and Lola would be asking for tastes."

Lola seemed to wake up more with the mention of samples. She climbed off the stool and lifted her cup high as she tossed back the last bits of coffee. She released a satisfied sigh and clinked the cup down on the counter like a drunken pirate slamming down his empty tankard in a tavern. "Let's get this production line going before I lose steam again."

Elsie continued to make the decorations as I dabbed royal icing onto the center of each cookie before pressing on the delicate fondant cut out. Lola was in charge of placing each individual cookie in a cellophane bag before tying it off with thin ribbon. The first souvenir cookie off the production line looked perfect.

"I'm going to charge double my usual cookie price for these," Elsie noted as she cut out a lighthouse. "Tourists tend not to mind the higher prices, and I need to make up for that calamity with the cinnamon rolls."

I dabbed some icing in the center of a cookie. "That sounds like a good business plan, Elsie."

Elsie held up the fondant lighthouse. "These really are cute. I'll have to save one for Marty Tate."

"That's the man who takes care of the lighthouse, right?" I asked.

Elsie's rounded eyes turned my direction. "You haven't met old Marty yet? He's a hoot."

"And as old as the great pyramids," Lola added. "How old is he, anyhow?" She glanced over at Elsie.

Elsie laughed. "That's sort of a running mystery in Port Danby. No one knows because for as long as anyone can remember Marty has been living in that little cottage and running the lighthouse. Kelly Dixon, over at the doctor's office, said her grandmother knew Marty as a kid and Kelly is no youngster. I'm guessing old Marty passed a hundred already."

I shook my head. "Wow, a century old. Hey, I wonder if Marty was around at the time of the Hawksworth murders." My shoulders deflated. "No, that would put him well into his hundreds."

"Guess you're still itching to research that old murder case." Elsie walked a tray of decorations over and set them down next to my work station. "Maybe you should ask Detective Briggs about it." She winked.

"What's that about, Elsie? Do you have something in your eye?" I flashed her a sarcastic grin. "Besides, I have asked Briggs about it, and he suggested I try the library. Which I plan to do whenever things slow down around this bustling town."

Elsie stretched her neck up to look outside. The pink and orange layers of dawn were just beginning to stripe the sky. "Looks like it's going to be a nice morning for the bloggers to set up."

"Yes, it looks that way." I passed a plate of finished cookies to Lola and stepped in to help her wrap them. "A few bloggers were already setting up yesterday. Do you know someone named Twyla Walton?"

Elsie stopped to tap her chin. "That name is so familiar. I had to leave the pastry chef class early because I pulled a tendon running in a marathon. Darn thing kept me off my feet for a month. I'd only taken the class to brush up on my techniques, so it wasn't a big deal to miss out on the last weeks." She cleared her throat. "Especially when I'd discovered that I knew more than the instructor."

"I'll bet you did. Twyla mentioned she had been a pastry chef. Her blog is Down Home Comfy and southern comfort food seems to be her specialty now."

"Yes, Twyla!" Elsie said enthusiastically enough to cause Lola to break the cookie she was sliding into the cellophane bag. Lola shrugged and ate the cookie.

Elsie continued. "I don't know how I could forget. It was such a big deal in the baking blogosphere, after all. I mean, it was all everyone talked about for months."

I cleared my throat to get her attention. "Care to fill us in on the details of this blogosphere whirlwind?"

Elsie wiped her hands clean on a towel and walked over to join us. "Twyla did attend pastry chef school. One of the projects, the last one I did before I got hurt, was to invent a new kind of donut. Twyla came up with a brilliant little puffed donut that was filled with chocolate hazelnut filling and then rolled in cinnamon sugar. They were incredibly tasty. A few years later, Marian Fitch, who had attended the same class, sold a recipe to a major donut chain. It was called the Hazelnut Bomb."

"Oh, I've had one of those," Lola mumbled over a mouthful of cookie. "They're the bomb. Get it?"

I raised a brow at her. "I guess we really did pull you out of bed too early." I turned back to Elsie. "Did Marian Fitch steal the recipe?"

"It was pretty much an exact copy, but by then Marian was already a big name with a bestselling cookbook and popular blog. Her lawyers squashed Twyla's case in court, and poor Twyla was stuck with Fitch's legal fees too. I think that's when she left the pastry world and moved to comfort food. Poor kid was devastated."

"Wow," Lola said with a shake of her head. "Don't you just hate it when the big guy wins and the little guy gets tromped on?"

"Yes," Elsie quickly agreed, "and if there is one big guy who needs some tromping, it's Marian Fitch." Elsie carried an empty tray over and filled it with the wrapped cookies. "I think I'll display these on the top shelf with a cute sign saying 'Don't leave without a sweet piece of Port Danby.'"

CHAPTER 5

*A*fter our extremely early morning in the bakery, my head felt a little heavy with fatigue. I went home for a quick hour nap before heading right back down Harbor Lane to help Yolanda at the Town Square.

Nearly all of the bloggers had arrived now and were hustling to make their booths attractive for tonight's opening dance. At least twenty booths had been set up along the entire border of the square where grass was planted in large rectangles to break up the cement walkways. The smattering of picnic tables that normally sat in the corners and through the center had all been moved into a cluster for fair attendees to sit with their food and drinks.

Some of the participants were lucky enough to get a booth under a shade tree. Although with autumn leaves falling faster than they could be picked up, it might have been better not to have the shade. Colorful, cleverly designed banners with blog names and logos fluttered along the fronts of the booths like a collection of mismatched skirts. As the treats and wares came out, the fair came alive with the promise of delicious bites and sips. At the 'French Confections' table, a multi-tiered display of pastel colored French macaroons sat next to a ceramic tray of tiny petit fours, each decorated with a fondant flower. In stark contrast, right next to it were the Barbecue Boyz, a pair of brothers who had an entire blog dedicated to great burgers and craft beer. They were setting up a massive grill, and their table was filled with a variety of barbecue sauces.

Dash had been wrangled by a persistent Yolanda into setting up heating lamps for tonight's dance. He was rolling a lamp's heavy base along the cement path as I parked my bicycle. I headed his direction.

"I see you can't say no to Yolanda either," I quipped. "Have you seen her? Or is she repainting the entire town before the fair guests arrive?"

"That woman does seem to have boundless energy. After all this, I'm ready to spend the rest of the weekend sitting in front of some video games."

I peered at him over my sunglasses. "I *thought* I heard an alarming amount of gun shots coming from inside your house. That along with a lot of loud arguing that seemed to have only one side, your side."

It was rare for Dash to look shy, but he had a sheepish grin on his face. "Guess I need to stop shouting at the games. Either that or insulate the walls better."

Yolanda dashed through my field of vision, like a scurrying mouse. "Oops, there's the boss. I guess I'll find out what she needs me to do. Catch you later. Unless maybe you'll be too tired for that dance."

"Not a chance, Pinkerton. You're not getting out of it that easy."

I shrugged. "Worth a try." I headed across the pathway. Only one booth was still vacant. It was double the size of the other booths.

"No, Trixie, you bad hen! Come back here!" a woman's voice was followed by a fat maroon feathered chicken scurrying across the lawn and path.

I crouched down and stopped its progress. The bird's red fleshy comb wobbled back and forth as it turned its head side to side to seek out an escape route. Fortunately, I had some skill with a headstrong bird.

"Look what I have," I said as I held out my empty palm.

The bird eyed the invisible treat and walked forward to investigate, giving her owner a chance to swoop in and grab the hen.

"Thank you. Trixie is such a scoundrel." She stuck out her hand. "Celeste Bower, I run a country living blog called 'Sweet Cherry Pie.'" Celeste looked to be about thirty, but it was hard to tell her age due to her flawless pink skin. She had big blue eyes. Her curly blonde hair was swept up on the sides and held in place by decorative clips. She was wearing a Tom Petty concert shirt that didn't really go with the rest of her, or a country blog, but I was instantly drawn to her purple cowboy boots.

"I'm Lacey and I love your boots."

She looked down at them and turned her ankle back and forth. "Aren't they great? I found them at a flea market." Trixie grew restless in her arm.

"I'll let you put the chicken away." I stretched up and looked past her to the booth with the Sweet Cherry Pie banner. "What a cute little chicken coop." Another chicken was scratching away at the grass under the coop.

"Yes and it's easy to transport. They have a much bigger coop at home, of course. It's like a chicken palace."

"That's wonderful. Well, I'll let you get back to your work. I'm sure you have plenty to do."

"Is Marian Fitch coming?" Celeste asked. "I haven't seen her. She's the headliner for the fair." The slightest eye roll followed.

"I'm not sure. Let me know if you need anything."

I reached Yolanda, who was just ripping open a cardboard box.

"Did someone cancel, Yolanda? I see an empty booth. And why is it a double?"

"No one cancelled. That is Marian Fitch's booth. She requested a double." Yolanda straightened from the box and handed me, of all things, a deflated beach ball.

I stared down at it. "I'm holding a flat beach ball."

"Yes. Would you be a dear and blow them up? I'm going to have Dash hang some from the trees. I thought they'd add a festive touch and remind everyone to check out Port Danby's wonderful beach."

"How many are there?" I was already feeling lightheaded from getting up in the middle of the night. I could only imagine how silly I would be after blowing up beach balls.

"There are only twenty." She didn't give me a chance to respond before something else caught her attention. "No, no, I don't want the speakers so close to the booths," she called to the workmen setting up the sound system. She hurried off, leaving me standing with a box of airless beach balls.

I decided to dump out the balls and turn the box over to the unopened side. I sat gently on it. It seemed I might have less chance of falling on my face from lack of oxygen if I sat to blow the balls up.

My vantage point gave me a clear view of the entire fair. It was coming along nicely. Yolanda could be proud.

After some coaxing, I got the first puffs of air into the beach ball. Dash was walking my direction, and I was bracing for him to tease me about my important job. I would simply remind him that at least I didn't have to climb up in trees and hang them.

I finished the first beach ball and realized quickly that I had no place to secure them if a breeze swept through. I held the first one between my feet and started on the second one. With my cheeks puffed out in a hamster-like manner, Dash winked at me and then turned to talk to none other than the cute country living blogger in the purple boots. And, I certainly didn't mind because Dash had the right to talk to anyone he liked. I told myself that twice while watching the two of them laugh about something.

I finished the second ball and looked around. Since the double booth was still vacant, I decided to toss the balls inside of it to avoid having to chase down and herd together a bunch of wayward beach balls.

Twyla's booth was across the way. She waved in between cutting some potatoes. "I don't envy you that job," she called.

"Thanks." I tossed the first two beach balls into the booth. Celeste's booth was right next door, and Dash was still being the overly friendly local, making small chat with her. Oh, who was I kidding? It wasn't small chat. It was flirting, something Dash was highly skilled at. Apparently Celeste was telling him all about the last Tom Petty concert she went to and how she and her sister were obsessed with his music.

With my beach balls secured, I headed back to my box to blow up a few more. This time I faced away from the fair and my overly friendly neighbor and admired the fall trees across the way.

I finished six more beach balls and decided I needed a break. I got up too suddenly. The autumn foliage swirled into a flame colored blur. I swayed forward and was close to pitching face first on the cement when a large hand took hold of my arm to steady me.

"Watch it. Those beach balls can be dangerous." I hadn't heard his voice in awhile. I realized I had missed it. His dark eyes were hidden by sunglasses, but his familiar half smile showed right up on cue. And then there was that perfect curl of hair on the back of his shirt collar.

"Detective Briggs? I didn't expect to see you here."

"I'm just here to ask Yolanda a few details about parking." He surveyed the beach balls I had yet to blow up. "Seems she has you busy too."

As he spoke, a large white box truck pulled up along the curb next to the park. A navy blue sedan pulled up behind it.

Yolanda hurried over. "Detective Briggs, you're here. I'm going to show you where we need the no parking cones." Yolanda, who already talked fast, was starting to sound like an auctioneer. "Oh my, there's Marian Fitch with her things." She took a breath. "After a few phone conversations with the woman, I'm not looking forward to meeting her." A visible shiver ran through Yolanda. "She's quite demanding. Come, Detective. Follow me."

Briggs shot me a small grin before he followed behind Yolanda. The two lines that creased his mouth when he smiled—I'd forgotten about those too.

My head was solid again as I bent down to pick up the next beach ball. Behind me, an angry voice broke the otherwise convivial atmosphere in the town square.

"Who put these ridiculous beach balls inside my booth?"

Seemed that so far everything I'd heard about Marian Fitch was spot on.

CHAPTER 6

$\mathcal{J}$t was amazing how the arrival of one small woman could turn a smooth running operation upside down. Marian Fitch, the fifty-something owner of the Sugar Lips company and blog had thick wavy hair, which she had dyed a severe black to contrast with a pasty white, heavily powdered complexion. The dark red lipstick, which was used to paint on a bow shape that didn't really exist, topped off the woman's stark color scheme. Her dark, deep set eyes were bordered by a pair of rectangle framed eyeglasses that made her eyes look extra big, reminding me of the 'why, Grandma, what big eyes you have' line in Red Riding Hood. She wore a slightly outdated satin blouse that she'd topped off with a long strand of pearls.

After the removal of my *highly inconvenient* beach balls, Marian Fitch took a sweeping look around and her bow shaped lips twisted into an angry pretzel. "This won't do," was all she said before screeching for her assistant.

Fitch's assistant turned out to be her obedient nephew, Parker Hermann. Parker was an anxious, jittery twenty-something, who wore his brown hair combed heavily to one side. He tucked his short sleeved, button down shirt, a camel colored cotton, into his pants and tied off the entire prim look, astonishingly enough, with a wide belt and big silver skull-shaped belt buckle. He was obviously fond of the buckle because he made a point of adjusting it every time he spoke. After watching him in action with his aunt berating him at every turn, I was feeling rather sorry for him just ten minutes into their arrival.

An hour into their arrival, the double booth had been deconstructed and reconstructed in a more suitable location, especially away from those smelly chickens. (Marian Fitch's words, not mine.)

I'd had about enough setting up for the day and needed to get back to my shop. I'd closed it for the entire morning, but I had plenty to do. Not to mention, I was sure Kingston would be pacing his perch, wondering where I'd disappeared to for so long.

As I headed toward Pickford Way, I saw Lester rolling a cart filled with lidded coffee cups. The wheels got caught on the lip of the cement, so I raced over to help him.

"Lacey, you're just in time. I decided to brew up some of my special dark roast and offer some to the fair participants."

"That was kind of you, Lester. I'll help you pass them out."

"Would you? Thanks so much. I even brought a few pitchers of cream and dairy free creamer."

I helped Lester navigate the busy lawn with his cart. The first stop was none other than the Sugar Lips booth. Parker was balancing on a chair trying to hang up a sign, while Marian busied herself with very little as she sat on a chair she'd brought along. I was surprised to see it wasn't painted gold and in the shape of a throne.

"Welcome to Port Danby," Lester said. He placed two cups of coffee on the wood shelf of the booth. Lester flashed Marian his gracious smile. As far as I was concerned, his was the kind of smile that could brighten even a rotten day, but the woman couldn't even work up a lip turn. Maybe she was worried she would ruin the clownish amount of lipstick she had smeared on her thin lips.

Lester was a little taken aback, so I jumped in to save him from the shark infested waters. I picked up the creamer. "Cream or non-dairy?" I asked cheerily.

Marian gave the creamer a cursory glance. "Neither. I have my own." She reached into her bag and pulled out a small white bottle with a French label. "I only use this creamer. I buy it whenever I'm in France. There is nothing else like it."

"France, wow. It must be delicious." Lester was great at pretending charm even when he wasn't feeling it.

Marian picked up the cup of coffee and read the label. "Coffee Hutch."

"Yes, indeed. I'm the owner. We're located just a few blocks away on—"

"If you own a coffee shop of any merit, then you should consider carrying this creamer."

Lester was stopped cold on his impromptu commercial. He snuck a glance my direction, and I snuck a wink back.

"He'll look into it," I said. "Well, Lester, maybe we should get moving before these coffees get cold."

"Yes," Lester said. "It's rather chilly out here in the town square." He winked back at me.

Suddenly a business card clutched in long white fingers that were topped in red nail polish was shoved in my face. "Here's my business card. It has my blog and website listed. I have several posts about the creamer and where to buy it."

"Right." I pushed the card into my pocket. "Thank you."

"Good day," Lester said through a tight jaw. We rolled the cart to the Barbecue Boyz booth. Lester leaned his head my direction. "Sugar lips? More like sourpuss."

I had to control my laughter, afraid that Fitch would think we were laughing at her.

Oh, that's right. We were.

CHAPTER 7

a loud clanging disintegrated the strange dream I was having about beach balls filled with coffee creamer. It took me more than a few seconds to figure out where I was and why my neck and back were so stiff. I lifted my heavy head from my forearms. My bottom wobbled on the stool beneath me. And through the fog of my heavy sleep, a dark figure walked toward me. The late afternoon sun coming through the windows blotted out his features.

"Miss Pinkerton, are you all right?"

I took a deep breath and slipped off the stool but fortunately landed on my feet. "Detective Briggs." My voice had that raspy, just woke up quality to it. I cleared my throat. "I must have dozed off." Between getting up early to help Elsie with her souvenir cookies and blowing up twenty beach balls, the day had finally caught up to me.

I looked over at Kingston's perch. It was empty. Then I remembered my irritated crow had flown right over me and out of the shop the second I opened the door.

"What are you doing here?" I asked. "Have you come to order one of my Thanksgiving centerpieces?"

He smiled and shook his head. "Actually, I heard that Elsie had made cinnamon rolls, so I decided to stop for one. But I'm a day too late. Then I walked past your shop and glanced in the window and saw you fast asleep with your head on the counter. I worried something was wrong, and here I am." He pointed up to his thick dark hair. "You have something right—"

I reached up and my fingers grazed over a stem of green fern. I yanked it free and tossed it onto the counter. "Must have fallen asleep on my work. Excuse me, I see a grumpy crow in the tree out front."

I opened the shop door and just as he had swooped angrily out of the store, Kingston swooped angrily back inside. He didn't even give Detective Briggs a cursory glance before flying straight to his perch. And Briggs, who was always cool as cream, hardly flinched as the big black crow swept past him.

I stretched my arms out and tried to ease the grogginess out of my head with a deep breath. "I think I'm going to need some fresh air."

"I'll walk with you. I was going to head to the beach and eat my lighthouse souvenir." He lifted up a cellophane wrapped cookie.

"You bought a souvenir cookie. Good for you. A quick jaunt to the beach works." It was rare for Detective Briggs to be so friendly and informal. I wasn't going to waste the opportunity. I grabbed my keys and sweatshirt and flipped over my closed sign, not that I expected any customers at the end of the day. Everyone was too busy getting ready for the dance.

We walked out onto the sidewalk. Yolanda's voice blasted out over the town saying 'testing one, two, three' over and over again. Each time her sound test was followed by a piercing, high pitched noise that made my shoulders bunch up to my ears.

Briggs laughed. "I guess they don't quite have the sound system perfected yet."

"Apparently not. Poor Yolanda. She's sounding a little on the edge of hysteria in those sound tests. She has worked so hard. I hope it all goes smoothly."

We headed past Franki's Diner and on to Pickford Way where we could catch the walkway down to the sand.

Briggs offered me a piece of cookie, which I declined, before he took a big bite, effectively removing the black pointed top of the lighthouse. His permanent five o'clock shadow was thick from a long day at work. I'd deduced that since he had to wear proper suits and shoes for work, the unshaven jaw and slightly long hair were his small concessions to a wilder side of James Briggs. Although, I might have been totally wrong. It was possible he was just as no-nonsense in his personal life.

"Will we be seeing the illustrious Detective Briggs at the dance tonight?"

"I don't know about that. Dances and fairs aren't exactly my thing."

"How disappointing. I was hoping I could show you just what a terrible dancer I am."

He laughed. "I confess, that would make it all worth it. But I doubt I'll be there."

I was surprised at how disappointed I felt about him not attending the dance. But I was being silly. I should have known James Briggs wasn't the town dance type.

"It's been a few weeks since I've seen you," I said. "Are there any big, exciting cases you've been working on? I've been itching for a new mystery to solve."

"Nothing too exciting. Mostly cut and dry cases. I thought you were going to do some research on the Hawksworth murder-suicide."

"I haven't had any time. But now that you mentioned it, I am planning to go up there and visit the little makeshift museum in the gardener's shed. It'll be open all weekend for visitors."

We reached the sand. Port Danby had been a bustling port back in the day when the Hawksworth Manor was in its glory. But bigger and more modern ports down south made Port Danby obsolete. The docks had been trimmed down to a marina for fishing and pleasure boats, and the shoreline had been smoothed into a nice beach for day trips.

"Yes, I've heard they're opening it. I just hope Officer Chinmoor and I don't have to pry any curious trespassers out from the broken stairway. I've had to do that several times."

"Really?" I asked adding in a hand gesture to my chest to show disbelief. "Wow, I guess some people just ignore those warning signs and climb right over the chain link fence and through those big front doors."

He looked at me for a moment, and the tiniest twinkle lit up his dark eyes. "Why, Miss Pinkerton, you just listed those details for trespassing so perfectly, I'd almost think you'd done it yourself."

Again with the chest touch. "Me? Never." I blinked a few times just to punctuate my innocence. "And I certainly had nothing to do with the inside doorknob breaking off. Nothing at all to do with that."

"That's reassuring to hear." Briggs tossed a few cookie crumbs to a lone seagull. Instantly, seagulls dropped out of the sky, screeching and clamoring to get a piece of the cookie. "By the way, the Chesterton Library has better information. They still have those old microfiche machines, believe it or not.""

"Somehow, I believe it." I put my arm up to ward off some of the winged chaos raining down over us. "Elsie is one heck of a baker. Even the gulls agree."

The briny sea air had revived me, and I needed to head back to the shop and lock up for the night. I now had a greater urge to visit the Hawksworth Manor. I was in need of some mystery. "This walk has certainly refreshed me. But I should head back."

"Me as well."

Briggs and I turned back up the path toward Harbor Lane. We stopped in front of the Port Danby Police Station. The black and white police cruiser wasn't parked out front.

"Where's Officer Chinmoor?"

"He went home early to get ready for the dance," Briggs said with an edge of amusement.

"Good for him. At least he's going to the dance." I shot him a pointed look.

Briggs ignored my pointed look. "Yes, he's been looking forward to it. Well, I'll let you know if I need that million dollar nose of yours for any cases, Miss Pinkerton. Thank you for the walk."

I tapped my nose. "Me and my trusty partner are ready for the call of duty anytime. Good afternoon, Detective Briggs."

"Good afternoon, Miss Pinkerton."

CHAPTER 8

$\mathcal{I}$t had been an interminably long day, what with getting up before dawn and then working down at the fair. And it was far from over. The town square would start filling up for the dance in just a few hours. I had to admit, I had little enthusiasm for the event. It was going to be a lot of noise and people and, as Elsie mentioned, chaos. And after my long day, curling up with my cat, hot cocoa and a good book sounded much more inviting. But I was still new enough to Port Danby that I had to show enthusiastic support for town activities.

On my way back to the flower shop, after my short, refreshing and unexpected walk with Detective Briggs, I'd stopped into the diner to make sure Franki's daughters were opening the gardener's shed for the afternoon. I was in luck. Franki had told me that Kimi and Kylie would be selling tickets until seven. They, of course, needed time to get ready for the dance. I knew there would be a big crowd up at the mansion for the rest of the weekend and decided this would probably be my only chance to look inside the *museum*.

I decided to walk the short distance up Maple Hill to the mansion. Pillows of gunmetal gray clouds cluttered the deep blue horizon, signaling that the fair might not get off to a sunny start tomorrow. I'd checked my phone more than once and no rain was forecast, but the little white cloud icon was covering the yellow sun. It was just as well. People were going to be there to eat and buy cookbooks. They weren't in Port Danby for sunning on the beach. Tanning season was long gone.

Extra signs warning visitors to not climb the fence or go inside the house had been posted. The last time I hiked the hill to the mansion had been during an early morning, last second decision. A heavy, dreary fog had shrouded the hill and the house, making it seem extra creepy. Tonight, under the moonlit sky and with the extra safety lights added on the path to the gardener's shed, the two tall turrets, pitched roofs and carved balustrades running along the porch and balcony looked far less sinister. Tonight, it looked more like a neglected old house than the notorious scene of a murder.

I could hear giggles as I rounded the side of the house, following lights and lit arrows to the main attraction, the Hawksworth Museum. The gardener's shed had most likely been built the same time as the house. The shed was actually a small, barn shaped building with sliding front doors and two squat windows on each side. Unlike the house, which was slowly withering away into dust, the town had spent time and money to replace rotted wood and keep a fresh coat of green paint on the facade. It looked sparkling new compared to the drab mansion behind it.

Bright lights had been set up in front of the entrance. Kimi and Kylie, Franki's fourteen-year-old identical twins were much easier to tell apart than their brothers, Taylor and Tyler. Especially since Kimi had decided to cut bangs in her shiny, toffee colored hair. Kylie had left hers long. They were both busy looking at something on a phone when I walked up.

Kimi looked up. "Pink! You're here." She hopped off her fold-up chair and ran to give me a hug. Along with Elsie and Lola, Franki was one of the people I'd quickly formed a strong friendship with, and I adored her kids. Kimi took my hand and led me to the wobbly table that had been set up with a cash box and a roll of pink carnival tickets. "We've only sold four tickets, and it's almost time to close."

I pulled my five dollar bill out. "There. Now you've sold five tickets."

Kylie pulled off a ticket and handed it to me. I stared at it on my palm. "Who should I give it to?"

They crumpled into simultaneous laughter. "That's what we were wondering," Kimi spurted between peals of laughter. "Yolanda told us to hand out tickets, so that's what we're doing."

"Then good for you for following directions. I'll just put this in my pocket and wander inside."

"Have fun," Kylie chirruped. "Oh, but could you kind of hurry? Kimi is going to crimp my hair before the dance."

"I promise to just take a quick look around so you can be properly crimped in time for the dance."

They giggled again as I walked into the shed. Gosh, I missed being fourteen . . . sort of.

Of course, it was a well known, sobering fact that five dollars was considered only a small amount of money these days, but upon first glance at the Hawksworth Manor Museum, it seemed more effort could have been put into the contents, organization and overall display. After all, the town had gone through the trouble of keeping up the structure. They could have at least added a few paragraphs of description with each artifact.

The shelves that held the items lined each side of the shed. The lighting was close to laughable. Admittedly, it was dark outside, but somehow, I'd expected more illumination. Most of the lighting ran down the center aisle of the shed, leaving very little glow for the historical pieces on display. The ill-placed lighting did give the entire place an earthy, macabre vibe. Two round topped, tufted armchairs, upholstered in faded gold damask fabric sat at the end of the shed. Strings of moonlight pierced some of the thin, open seams between the wood plank siding, giving the chairs a ghostly appearance. I could almost see a staid, grim-faced Victorian couple sitting on the chairs, watching with blank stares as people eyed their possessions. A small shiver raced through me, and I gave my upper body a shake to rid myself of the feeling.

A pair of worn black lace up boots were the first item on the shelf. "Believed to be worn by Phoebe Hawksworth, the eldest of the three children," was what the one line summary stated. I blew a puff of air.

"Believed to be? Someone was just guessing," I muttered. My own voice came back to me in the shadowy room. Someone had taken the time to mount several glittery hat pins in a glass box. The label only said 'hat pins'. I guess I could assume they didn't belong to Bertram Hawksworth. A non-descript copper kettle with some patina from use sat next to the hat pins. Its use was obvious, but there was no mention of where it was found or what it had to do with the family's murder. A tall copper coal basket sat next to the kettle. They were both items that could have easily been sitting in Lola's Antique shop. Again, no mention of their connection to the crime. I was beginning to realize that the shed was just a collection of items from the house. I turned and walked down the back side of the building where an interesting collection of vintage garden tools was mounted as if someone had just been using them. I would have been interested to hear more about the infamous gardener of the estate, since he had been indicated as a motive for the murder. But there was no mention of him. Not even a picture of him with the odd, round handled spade or the funny trowel that looked more like a knife than a digging tool.

I turned away from the gardening display and gasped as I stared into a pair of lifeless eyes. A porcelain doll, with only one shoe and painted on hair, stared back at me from her shelf. The black pupils and most of the blue of her eyes had been erased, giving the doll a frightful gray stare. A toy rocking horse that was decaying in the moisture of the shed still had most of its mane and tail. Back then they used real horse hair, which was thick and durable and could apparently stand the test of time.

I gasped once more as a familiar beak pointed at me. Taxidermy was quite popular in Victorian times. People even had their dogs and horses stuffed. It seemed the Hawksworth family (perhaps due to their surname) were interested in birds. The stuffed crow and owl both still had a remarkable amount of plumage left. The crow made me shiver again.

I'd had enough of my museum visit. I turned toward the exit and noticed a large trunk beneath one of the shelves. I crouched down in front of it and pulled on the rusted lock, but it didn't budge.

Kimi and Kylie were folding up their chairs none too subtly. It was my cue to leave.

I helped them carry the table into the shed. "What's in that old trunk under the last shelf?" I asked.

"I don't know if it's ever been opened. Not sure why they bothered to put it there. I've heard it was the hope chest for the eldest daughter. Sheets and bedding and things for when she got married. Lot of good that hope chest did her," Kimi said before abruptly changing to a subject of greater interest. "Are you wearing your new boots tonight, Pink? My mom said you bought a slick new pair of go-go boots from the Mod Frock."

"I hadn't really given it much thought." We turned off the lights and slid shut the door. "Maybe I will."

Kylie put on the padlock. She patted the pocket of her sweatshirt and pulled out several old pictures. "Darn it, I forgot to put these back. They kept blowing off the wall."

I took hold of the pictures and squinted at them under the light on the front of the shed. They were old brown and white, faded pictures of people dressed in early twentieth century garb. "Is this the Hawksworth family?"

"Yep," Kimi said. "But I warn you, the last picture is creepy. It's the one the police took of the murder scene. I hate to look at it."

The light was poor, but I could see a faded image of two people stretched out on the floor in the same room I'd snuck into that foggy morning, the room with the green painted paneling and the piano. "Can I take these home to get a closer look?"

"Doesn't bother us," Kylie said with a shrug. "Can't keep those darn things on the wall anyhow. And everyone is more interested in the creepy stuff like the birds and the doll." Kylie put her hand over her mouth. "Oh my gosh. We should have warned you about the dead crow. I hope it didn't bother you too much."

"Not at all. But I do prefer live crows to stuffed ones."

We walked down the pathway together. "Especially when they're cool like Kingston," Kimi added.

Headlights circled over the property as a car came up the hill. "There's Mom. Come on, Kylie. We've got to get ready for the dance. See you there, Pink. Hey, do you want a ride down?"

"Nope, I'm fine. And thanks for lending me the pictures." I pushed the photos into the pocket of my sweatshirt and headed downhill to home.

CHAPTER 9

$\mathcal{T}$he strands of gold lights Dash had strung swayed lightly in the breeze, making all the shadows sway along with them. The glow reflected off the white canopy tops on the fair booths. The fountain that I had yet to see running with water had been filled with blue and pink balloons, giving them the look of giant colorful bubbles. A sparkling drink waterfall gurgled with pink lemonade next to a mouthwatering display of fair treats. The center of the square, which was mostly cracked and worn cement, had been covered with dark pieces of laminate, creating a makeshift dance floor. Speakers dangled from the lampposts blasting out every form of music from soft rock to country. All danceable tunes if the partner was right. And if my mod boots hadn't been killing my feet.

Lester wiped his face with his napkin attempting to erase the smudge of barbecue sauce. The song ended and Lola walked off the dance floor with Marian Fitch's nephew, Parker. I knew he wasn't even close to her type, but there just weren't that many unattached men for dance partners. The one person I'd planned to dance with, my highly popular neighbor, had been snagged long before I arrived at the dance. Kate Yardley, the owner of Mod Frock Vintage Boutique, had barely let Dash out of her sight all night. I was somewhat relieved not to have to dance. My nose might have been *super*, but my dance moves, not so much.

Elsie walked over with a coconut cupcake from the Cupcake Trolley booth. Apparently, back home in Indiana, Carla and Diane were the masters of the cupcake world. They had even expanded their business into a mobile bakery with a cupcake truck.

Elsie made a face as she took a bite of the cake. (It wasn't a hmm, that's delicious face.) "Dry crumb and the frosting leaves a film on the top of my mouth." She rolled her eyes. "Cupcake masters, indeed."

Lester folded up his grease stained paper plate. "Well, those Barbecue Boyz are talented. And I think Lola has her sights set on the one with the handlebar moustache."

The three of us glanced the direction of the barbecue booth. Lester might have been right in his assessment. After leaving the dance floor with Parker, my somewhat boy crazy friend had gone straight back to the Barbecue Boyz.

"Look who's talking," Elsie quipped. "You've had so many of those ribs, I'm just waiting for you to ask those boys to move to town."

"Do you think they'd consider it?" Lester asked.

Elsie waved her hand at him. "And you have all kinds of sauce on your chin. I should have brought some wet wipes with me."

"Ah ha, that reminds me." Lester dug something out of his pocket. He held up the square packet with the Barbecue Boyz logo. "These boys are genius. They even have their own wet wipes." He ripped it open and rubbed it on his chin. "How come you aren't dancing, Lacey?"

I looked pointedly down at my shiny black boots. They were perfectly mod and sixties in every way, and they sure had looked wonderful in the shop window. "Because, Les, I lost feeling in all ten toes about thirty minutes after I zipped these boots on. I guess I should have given them a longer test drive in the store."

"But you look adorable in that mini skirt and boots, Pink," Elsie noted. "If that makes you feel any better about the purchase."

"It does. And as long as I survive the night without losing any toes, I might even wear them again. Just not to a dance."

Lola tore herself away from the barbecue booth to come say hello. "You need to dance, Pink," she insisted. "There's some good music. You should just walk right up to Dash and steal him away from Kate. She's been glued to him all night."

"Nope, I'm fine right here, Lola. How was the dance with Parker?"

"Who? Oh, him. I feel bad for him. His aunt is a tyrant." Lola squeezed her voice to a harsh angry sound to mimic the aunt. "Parker, do this. Parker, do that. Parker, you're doing that all wrong. She even told him he was clumsy on the dance floor right in front of me. I thought the poor guy would melt into a puddle right there in front of the Sugar Lips banner."

"Yep, that's the woman I remember from pastry school," Elsie said. She squinted at something across the way. "And speaking of the pastry school reunion, it looks like Twyla Walton has visited the craft beer section of the barbecue booth once too often. Dash is having to help her off the dance floor."

Elsie's assessment seemed about right. Twyla looked a little unbalanced. Dash was politely leading her off the floor before she landed on her face. He wasn't two feet away from Twyla when Celeste Bower of Sweet Cherry Pie grabbed his arm for a dance.

"Well, he is the finest man out here," Lola noted.

I sighed. "I suppose." My gaze swept around for about the tenth time that evening hoping to catch a glimpse of Detective Briggs. It seemed he'd kept true to his word and stayed away from the dance.

"Looking for someone," Elsie asked in that tone that assured me she knew exactly who.

"Nope, just taking in the grand splendor of it all. Yolanda did a great job. I think this weekend is going to go very smoothly."

"I agree," Elsie said. "I wasn't too sure at first, but as long as the weather holds, it should be a great event."

Just as she finished her statement, an angry yell rang out during the lull between songs. Our curious gazes followed the voice. Twyla was standing in front of the Sugar Lips booth pointing angrily at Marian Fitch. Fitch sat calmly, a mask of ice, as she listened to Twyla's rant. "You stole my recipe and I will never forgive you! Shame on you,

Marian Fitch. You couldn't bake your way out of a donut hole. Your cookbook is a fake."

An awkward silence had swept through the crowd as all attention turned to the thin, red haired woman in the green dress. My feet moved her direction before my mind had even told me to do so. Twyla had had too much beer, and she was going to regret this scene tomorrow. I decided to cut it short, for her sake. And because the woman she was scolding couldn't have cared less. But before I reached Twyla, the tall handsome center of all the women's attention had rushed to her side. Dash was, as always, chivalrous, and as he led Twyla away from the scene, I could almost hear every woman in the square release a dreamy sigh.

I headed back. My services were not needed.

The music started up again, but the early guitar strums were drowned out by the rumble of a motorcycle. We turned in the direction of the noise.

The motorcycle rider stopped and climbed off the bike. There was something about the way he walked in his black motorcycle boots that seemed oddly familiar. He took off his helmet. I sucked in a quiet, little breath.

"Oh my gosh." I could smell the barbecue sauce on Lola's breath as she spoke. "Detective Briggs in jeans and a black shirt and riding a motorcycle. Heart be still. Who knew he had a wild side?"

I did, I said inside my head.

A hand wrapped around mine, and I was swung the opposite direction. Dash bowed down low. "Milady, we still have not had that dance you promised me."

"I don't know, Dash. My toes are kind of numb and . . ." I stopped talking because it seemed he wasn't taking any excuses.

Dash pulled me along to the floor. I wasn't three painful steps into the dance when I heard the motorcycle roar back to life. Its shiny chrome fenders glinted under the street lights as the motorcycle turned the corner and took off along Culpepper Road.

CHAPTER 10

$\mathcal{M}$y last customer walked out. I was sure I wouldn't have much business for the weekend, but I'd had a steady stream of people all morning. People from neighboring towns were planning ahead for the holidays. And I had a stack of orders for winter bouquets. After my tenth order, it dawned on me that I had to find an assistant who could also do local deliveries. I had never planned to do much commerce any farther than a fifty mile radius, but even for a small operation like mine, it seemed I was going to need some help.

I was scribbling out a help wanted ad to post after the busy weekend when Lola cruised into the store. "The food smells have penetrated every dusty corner of the antique shop. I have a hankering for something tasty. I see the customer rush has slowed on this side too. Why don't we stroll down to the fair and see what's cooking."

I put down my pen. "Or grilling? Which of the two Barbecue Boyz do you have your sights set on?"

She walked with heavy, disappointed steps to the counter. "Neither. They are both a couple of goobers, and they smell like ketchup and charcoal."

I grabbed my wallet and my keys. Kingston let out a low squawk signaling that he needed to go out. "Let's go, buddy. And no harassing people at the fair or you'll be staying home the rest of the weekend."

I opened the door. Kingston left behind a few downy feathers as he soared outside.

"You do realize that you talk to that crow as if he understands English," Lola mentioned on our way out the door.

"Not sure what your point is."

"No point, I suppose. I guess I talk to Bloomer the same way."

We turned toward Pickford Way. Cones had been set up for designated parking along Harbor Lane, Pickford Way and Culpepper Road. It seemed every available spot was taken. The roaring murmur of voices could be heard all the way down the street. Thin white trails of smoke, laden with rich fragrances, curled around the thinning branches of the trees. The fair was a success.

Lola wrapped her arm around mine. "Sooo, are you going to talk about the incident, or are you going to pretend it didn't happen?"

I looked over at her. She gazed back with an expectant smile.

"I have no idea what incident you're talking about."

She released my arm with a frustrated huff. "Sometimes you are so aggravating. The handsome, cool detective shows up to the dance on his shiny, silver and black motorcycle, no less, and the moment the dashing, charming neighbor drags you off to the dance floor, handsome, cool detective climbs back onto shiny, silver and black motorcycle and roars off into the night. Any of that scenario sound familiar?"

"I remember it, but I don't think it had anything to do with me."

We crossed the street. Detective Briggs' car was parked outside of the station. It seemed he was working this weekend. Most likely because of the fair. After I saw Briggs ride off, I briefly wondered if he'd done so because of me. But it was silly and vain of me to even entertain the notion. I was sure Briggs saw how crowded it was and decided not to stay.

I hadn't noticed Lola shaking her head at first. "Oh, Pink, you have a lot to learn about men."

"Said the woman who nearly gave her heart over to one of two men who smelled like ketchup and charcoal."

"Oh please, that crush lasted all of three songs at the fair and then I was over it."

We stopped at the entrance to the town square. After a morning of clouds and coastal breezes, the sun had arrived. But the booths and the participants all looked a little more weather worn than the night before.

The longest line was at the Sugar Lips booth where people waited patiently with their copies of Marian Fitch's cookbook. She was wearing a disingenuous grin as she hastily scrawled her name inside each book. I wondered how many of her fans felt a little less enamored with her once they met her in person. Her nephew stood nearby selling more copies of the book. They were the one booth with little to offer in samples and treats. It seemed they were all about profit. Not surprising.

"I want to try one of those hoagie sandwiches at the Sandwich Queen booth, and I've heard that Down Home Comfy has amazing sweet potato fries." Lola had her menu already picked, which with all the tempting choices was probably a good idea. Otherwise, I could very well spend my entire break just trying to decide.

Even with the crush of people in the square, I noticed Kingston's shadow pass overhead. I squinted up to the sky and watched my clever and scheming bird land gracefully on a thin branch. Four smaller birds took off in a hurry with the arrival of their big menacing nemesis. I quickly scanned the crowd for hats with fake fruits or nuts to make sure he wasn't planning to nibble on someone, but I saw nothing that could attract his attention. Especially because he had already zeroed in on something down below. The tree he'd landed on was directly over Celeste Bower's Sweet Cherry Pie booth. I could hear her two chickens clucking up a storm and hoped Kingston wasn't the cause of it.

"Go ahead and get your sandwich, Lola. I need to see what my bird is up to. I'll meet you at Twyla's booth for sweet potato fries."

Lola waved and was instantly swallowed up by the crowd. I made my way to Celeste's booth and casually glanced up to give my bird a scornful look. Kingston stared straight down at me and then I saw his shiny black eyes focus on a bag of grain that Celeste was holding. It must have been something tasty for chickens because they, too, were dancing and strutting in excitement.

Celeste stuck her nose in the bag and made a funny face. She tossed the entire bag into the trash she had set up below her stand. She noticed me watching her with interest. "Flax seed. It goes bad fast. The chickens love it, and it makes the eggs higher in nutritional value. Fortunately, I brought a second bag."

"Yes, I can see they love it." I smiled cheerily at her chickens and then scowled back up at my bird. I shook my head once at him, and he seemed to understand. I hoped.

"Have you sampled my honey lavender hand lotion?" Celeste's eyes were round and a clear sapphire blue. No wonder Dash had danced several dances with her. Not that I was counting.

"I haven't." I held out my palm and instantly knew the lotion was going to be far too strong for my sensitive nose, but I decided to be polite. She squirted in a dollop, and I rubbed it over my hands. "It's silky."

She handed me a card. "Everyone loves it. I've already sold out of the bottles I brought with me, but you can order more from my site."

"Great. Thanks." I pushed the card back into my pocket and took another glance up to the tree top. This time Celeste noticed my interest in the branches above her head.

"Go away, crow. You're scaring my chickens." Celeste flailed her hands, which, if I knew my bird, he was silently laughing at the woman and her useless antics. I decided to help her out.

I waved my hand sharply and gave Kingston another scowl. Reluctantly he lifted off the branch, leaving a waterfall of leaves behind as he flew away.

I breathed a sigh of relief that my pet wouldn't be making a ruckus at the fair. Things had been going so smoothly, I certainly didn't want to be the person to throw a wrench in it.

I moved through the crowd. Lola met me with a paper cone filled with sweet potato fries. "Try one," she said. "They have a spicy coating. They don't need ketchup." She held up a crispy, brown sphere on a napkin. "This is one of her deep fried peanut butter balls. I can't wait to try it."

I plucked out a long, hot fry and tasted it. "Hmm, if I could taste them over the honey, lavender smell on my hands, I'd bet the fries were delicious."

"Ah, so you sampled the hand lotion. I thought it was a little too fragrant."

"I agree." I tilted to the side and craned my neck to catch a glimpse of Twyla. She still looked her usual tense, uptight self, but it seemed she'd put the scene with Fitch behind her to have a successful fair day. People were lined up for her samples.

"What are you looking at?" Lola pushed another sweet potato fry between her lips.

"Just wondering how Twyla was doing after her little rant at the dance. Seems she's gotten over it. And the craft beer." I turned back to her. "I'm going to grab one of those peach smoothies at the vegan stand and then head back to the shop. How about you?"

Lola nodded absently. Her attention had been pulled away by the triple display of French pastries. "I think I'll stay here for a little longer and sample goodies."

"All right. See you later."

CHAPTER 11

*L*ester had been dragging around all day after overindulging on barbecued short ribs the night before. Robyn, his part-time coffee barista, had left early for a date, and I'd volunteered to remove and bring inside the cushions from the outside chairs so he could go home. I had just finished up and was about to head back to my own shop to clean up for the night when I saw Detective Briggs walk out of the station and toward the food fair.

I had no real reason for catching up to him other than I enjoyed talking to him. It was so rare when he had free time. And, of course, I was dying to ask him about the motorcycle. I'd gone over what Lola had said a few times in my head, but I was convinced he hadn't turned around and left because I'd gone off to dance with Dash. While it was true the two men seemed to dislike each other immensely, I was sure the dance had nothing to do with Briggs leaving. He'd told me himself that fairs and dances weren't his thing. I was sure he was put off by the packed, boisterous crowd he saw in the square.

I hurried along the sidewalk after successfully walking past Lola's Antiques without my nosy friend popping out to see where I was going. I didn't need her making up conclusions about my race down the street to catch up with Detective Briggs. Besides, it wasn't really a race. It was more of a speed walk.

I rounded the corner on Pickford Way and wasn't too surprised to see that most of the booths had closed up for the night. Barbecue Boyz, Sandwich Queen and DAB, the vegan booth, were the only participants left. Even Celeste's two hens had gone in for the night. The sun was dropping low in the sky, and the fair would close up officially before dark. Most of the visitors had filled themselves to their eyeballs with sugary treats, savory meats and all the goodies that didn't fit into a normal food category.

The Barbecue Boyz had turned off the grills, but there were still several trays of burgers displayed at their booth. That was where I found Briggs handing over money for a cheeseburger.

He was just about to take a bite when he saw me.

"Don't let me stop you," I said cheerily. "I hear their burgers are delicious."

Detective Briggs chewed and swallowed. "Very good. This was the first chance I had to visit the fair today. Guess I missed most of the vendors. But I probably still would have chosen the burger."

I walked with him toward the cluster of tables. Yolanda had paid some of the high school kids to clean up trash in the afternoon. Taylor and Tyler, Franki's twin sons, were amongst the helpers.

"Yolanda thought of everything," Briggs remarked as we sat at a table. It was probably the first time the benches had been empty all day.

"You might not have had many food choices, but I can assure you there was no place to sit or hardly even stand just a few hours ago. You were wise to wait."

"No choice. I was buried under a mound of paperwork. The worst, most tedious part of my job." He took another bite and opened the water bottle he'd brought along.

"Mine too. Not that I'm comparing flower arranger to police detective, but I hate the paperwork that goes along with the business. If I could, I'd just spend all my time with the flowers. And I'm sure you'd prefer to spend all your time with the—" I stopped. I'd talked myself into a corner, not sure how to fill in the blank.

Briggs smiled as he swallowed. "Dead bodies?" he finished for me.

"I suppose I started that analogy and didn't think about where it led for your line of work. Anyhow, I'll change the subject so my cheeks can cool down from the embarrassed blush." I switched topics too hastily without thinking it through. "Where did you ride off to so quickly last night? And how come you never mentioned you had a motorcycle?"

Briggs looked a little put off by my questions. He took another bite of burger and gazed out at the coastline and the lighthouse. I was almost convinced he wasn't going to answer, which would have made me feel even sillier than a few minutes earlier. Then he swallowed and took a long sip of water.

"I was out for a ride on my motorcycle." He tilted his head my direction. "Which I didn't know I was required to mention, so I apologize for that indiscretion."

"Apology accepted as long as I can have a ride on it someday."

A slight grin appeared behind his napkin as he wiped his mouth. "Anyhow, I was mostly checking to see if parking and fire codes were being followed."

"Detective Briggs, the code enforcer," I chirped.

He ignored my tease. "It was so crowded, I decided not to stay."

I shouldn't have been disappointed in his reason for leaving, but deep down, it was possible I wanted Lola to be just a little bit right.

"Yes, it was terribly crowded. I'd made a bad choice on foot attire, and my feet were too sore for the dance floor."

"Oh, is that right? Thought I saw you dancing with Vanhouten." He said the name with more than a smattering of derision.

I lifted a brow at him. "You certainly are a good detective. You weren't off your bike for two minutes, yet you knew that I'd danced with Dash."

Rather than verbally agree with my assessment, he just nodded as he took a large bite of burger.

"If you'd stuck around long enough, you would have also seen that

I ended the dance early in the song. Not because of my dance partner. Dash is a very talented dancer. And chivalrous."

Briggs didn't say any more. I was stupid for needling him with more details. I knew darn well he didn't care for Dash.

It seemed I'd overstayed my welcome. "I guess I should head back to the shop. I've got a few things to do before I close up for the night."

He drank his food down with a swallow of water. "It was nice talking with you, Miss Pinkerton."

"You too." I climbed off the bench just as tires shrieked to a stop in the distance.

Briggs and I both looked down the long aisle of food booths. The black and white police car had stopped on Pickford Way. Officer Chinmoor, Briggs' young and slightly goofy partner at the police station, came lumbering across the grass. He was holding up his two way radio.

"I tried to call you," he said urgently. Even with his partner striding across the square as if his hair was on fire, Briggs kept his cool. He took his radio off his belt and turned up the volume.

"Just wanted to unplug while I ate my lunch," he told Chinmoor. "What has you huffing and puffing?"

Officer Chinmoor stopped to catch his breath. "There's a body, a dead body. At the Mayfield Hotel. The medics are there, and they say the woman is dead. What should I tell them?"

Briggs wrapped up what was left of the burger and wiped his hands. "Tell them I'm on my way."

"Right." Officer Chinmoor walked away on his long, gangly legs, talking into his radio as he went.

I kept my eager grin hidden as Briggs stood from the table. "Why are you grinning at me, Pinkerton?"

"I thought I was hiding it."

"Nope." He pointed to the corner of my mouth. "I can see the little curl right there."

"I was just thinking that it's been awhile since we were on a case together."

"We were never on a case together."

I put my hands on my hips and sighed loudly. "You needed me and my nose for Beverly Kent's murder."

"That's true."

"What if you need me and my nose this time? Couldn't I just drive along with you? I'll stay out of your way and just sniff around."

"It might just be a natural death."

I blinked at him and smiled weakly.

His sigh of surrender bordered on a grunt. "Fine. You can come along. But don't get in the way."

I hurried along next to him. "Nope, you won't even know I'm there."

"Somehow I doubt that."

CHAPTER 12

A cluster of emergency vehicles were parked at the lobby entrance of the Mayfield Hotel. I'd seen the gray roof of the multistory hotel just in passing on my way through Mayfield, but this was the first time I'd seen the hotel in its entirety. It looked to be an older building but with fresh white balconies outside each window. The long portico leading to the glass doors of the lobby was held up by thick white columns. Billowy, feathery asparagus ferns cascaded from the hanging baskets along each side of the portico.

On the drive to Mayfield, Detective Briggs had been in constant contact with an officer on the scene. He had no time for idol chat with his tag along passenger. He was in full detective mode by the time we stepped out of the car. The officer, an Officer Pritchett, was from the Mayfield Police Department, but she seemed to know Briggs well as she filled him in on the radio. Apparently we were about to arrive at a scene where a woman had mysteriously dropped dead in her hotel room. My few years of medical school had not ended in a medical degree, (much to the dismay of my mom) but they had prepared me to see dead bodies without the usual squeamish or shocked reaction of most people.

Briggs had let Officer Pritchett know that he was heading into the lobby as we climbed out of the car. I decided to remain as invisible as possible while he conducted his official business.

We stepped into the hotel lobby. A frazzled looking gentleman with a tuft of gray hair combed over his otherwise bald head was dashing back and forth in the lobby, barking orders at employees. His forehead was deep with lines of worry. I couldn't read the small gold badge on his suit pocket, but I was pretty sure it said 'manager'.

A few confused and stunned guests stood in the lobby with their suitcases, watching the flurry of activity and the parade of medics and firemen streaming in and out of the elevator. And to top off all the chaos, an elevator repairman was busy working on the control panel sitting between two of the visitor lifts. I could only imagine, by the harried state of the manager, that death was not a normal event at the hotel.

The elevator marked 'staff only' opened, and a young police woman with thick copper hair, green eyes and just a touch too much pink blush strolled over in her uniform. She managed to make the dull blue slacks and shirt look as if they could be worn on the runway. I shouldn't have felt disappointed (and a bit dowdy) upon seeing the beautiful female officer, but I did.

"Detective Briggs, I'll show you up to the room." She glanced at me.

"Miss Pinkerton is with me," Briggs said quickly and then just as quickly headed to the service elevator.

The three of us stood in a moment of awkward silence as the elevator shimmied up toward the eighth floor.

"It's one of the suite rooms." Officer Pritchett seemed to decide that it was all right to talk in front of me. "The woman was one of the food bloggers from the fair in Port Danby. According to the manager, Mr. Trumble, the frantic looking man you saw in the lobby, a number of the rooms have been rented by participants and visitors to the food fair." She reached over and tapped his arm. "Guess they didn't want to stay at the run-down motel on Pickford Way."

I was about to speak up and defend the Port Danby Motel, even though it was a touch run-down, but I decided since I was standing in the middle of police business and I didn't actually belong there, I'd just keep to my invisibility plan.

The elevator stopped and we stepped off and headed left. Several policemen were standing outside Suite 801. They opened the door and let us through.

A crystal chandelier glittered overhead as we moved past an officer and a medic. Another policeman was standing with his back to us consoling someone in the center of the sunken in seating area, which was filled with an ivory colored sectional, glass end tables and afforded a panoramic view of the ocean.

The officer turned when he heard Detective Briggs' voice, giving me a clear view of the person he had been consoling. Parker Hermann. His face was pale, and it seemed he had been crying. But not too much. He was wringing his hands as he saw more people enter the room.

There was a book on the counter beneath the television. It was a Sugar Lips Cookbook, confirming my suspicions. We were in Marian Fitch's room.

Officer Pritchett led us down the short hallway, past a gloriously appointed bathroom that sparkled with marble and chrome. She stopped at the entrance to a bedroom and looked pointedly at me and then at Briggs.

"Miss Pinkerton can come in too."

I shouldn't have been so thrilled. We were, after all, about to walk into a room with a dead body, but I had to hold my grin back.

We walked into the bedroom. Marian Fitch was sprawled out on the bed with her legs hanging over the side. Her eyes were wide open, never a good look for a dead person, especially for a woman with severe black hair and a powdered white complexion. I couldn't help but notice that she looked a bit vampire-ish. It sent a chill through me.

Briggs who had an uncanny ability to sense even my smallest reactions turned with a curled brow. "Are you all right?"

"Yes. I'm fine."

Officer Pritchett listed some details as I browsed the room. The phone was off the hook as if she had been trying to call for help. A cup of coffee, a hotel cup, sat on the nightstand by the bed. It had spilled, and the brown liquid was dripping off the shiny nightstand. Next to the spilled cup was Marian Fitch's special coffee creamer.

"There are no signs of injury," Pritchett spoke behind me. Her voice had a sultry edge to it. Darn her. "Mr. Trumble, the hotel manager, said someone from this room had called down at four o'clock to order a cup of coffee to be brought to the room at five."

"Strange," Briggs said. "Why the hour delay?"

"There's an explanation for that," Pritchett piped up. "The hotel offers free coffee and tea from five until six. Apparently, their coffee brew is considered the best in the area."

A snort of derision shot out before I could stop it. I'd gotten their attention. "Sorry, it's just that the Coffee Hutch already has that honor. But please, continue."

I heard a quiet mumble behind me as if Pritchett was asking about me. Briggs muttered a short response.

The officer walked into the bedroom with Parker Hermann. "Please," Parker said, "I just need to be with my aunt. What happened to her? I'm surrounded by police and medics and not one person can answer that."

Perhaps a bit of his aunt had rubbed off on him.

"We are trying to assess that, Mr.—" Briggs stopped and let the officer fill him in on the name.

"This is Parker Hermann," Pritchett said. "He is Ms. Fitch's nephew. He travels with her and works as her assistant."

"Or at least I did." He covered his face in despair. It seemed mostly genuine.

As I turned back to the coffee, I smelled something that wasn't entirely coffee, or creamer, for that matter.

I leaned over to get a whiff.

"Don't touch anything," Officer Pritchett snapped.

"Just breathing in the air," I said with a pleasant smile.

"Do you smell something out of the ordinary?" Briggs asked as he walked over.

"Yes, out of the ordinary for a cup of coffee." I straightened, and it seemed all eyes, even Parker's, were on me.

"Peanut butter," I said. "I think it's in the creamer."

Parker's mouth dropped open. "That's impossible. My aunt has a deadly peanut allergy. One taste of peanut and she goes into anaphylactic shock. There are no peanuts in that creamer. She's been drinking it for years."

Briggs looked at me and then at the body on the bed. "Miss Pinkerton, would you be able to smell the peanut butter on the victim's mouth?"

"Possibly." I walked over and knelt gently on the bed, trying to avoid Marian's direct, lifeless stare as I leaned down to her face. One quick whiff told me everything I needed to know. I climbed back off the bed, and as I did so, Marian's hand rolled off her body and bounced on the quilt covered mattress like rubber.

The other people in the room looked baffled and more than a little skeptical as they waited for my conclusion.

I turned to Briggs. "Definitely peanut butter."

CHAPTER 13

*M*arian Fitch lay still on the bed with her wide-eyed stunned expression. It seemed clear now that the reason her eyes were wide and one hand was on her chest was that her throat had constricted in a fatal allergic reaction to peanuts. For some people, the innocent, funny little nut that came two to a shell and that people gobbled down at baseball games and bars was as toxic as the worst kind of poison. According to her nephew, Parker, Marian had been one of those people.

Parker shook his head in disbelief after I emphatically stated that the creamer contained peanuts. Of course, why should he believe a stranger? He knew nothing of my hyperosmia, my extreme sense of smell. But there was no doubt in my nose or my mind that the creamer had a smidgen of peanut butter in it.

Parker pushed past me and lunged forward to reach for the creamer.

"Don't touch that," Detective Briggs said sharply.

Parker froze as if someone had just sprayed him with dry ice. He shot Briggs an irritated glare.

"We are going to need it for evidence and fingerprints," Briggs explained.

"Evidence?" Parker's face morphed from irritation to shock.

Briggs seemed to be assessing his reaction. I'd already discovered that Detective James Briggs was one of those quiet, introspective types, who was great at finding clues in people's reactions. "Yes, evidence, Mr. Hermann. Unless you think your aunt poisoned herself with peanut butter, it seems someone purposely laced the creamer. Someone who wanted to see her dead."

"But this is all ridiculous." Parker popped out of his stunned state. "Aunt Marian has an epinephrine pen. She carries it with her wherever she goes. It's probably sitting right there in her purse for emergencies. We're both well trained on how to use it." Parker walked into the master bathroom and returned. "I don't see the pen, so it must still be in her purse." He skirted around his aunt's legs. I noted how he hardly gave her a second glance as he passed. It seemed the shock of her death had already worn off.

Parker walked over to two pieces of designer luggage. He tilted each one side to side. "That's odd. She always puts her purse next to the suit—" He fell silent and his face grew white. It took him a second to speak, especially with three police officers staring at him. "I put it inside the safe in the closet. She usually pulls the pen out." His steps were a little less confident as he headed to the closet. He pulled a piece of paper out and used the numbers written there to open the safe. He pulled the purse from the safe as if it was filled with explosives. The pale pink pallor of his skin tinged with gray as he took the epinephrine pen out. "I thought she'd pulled it out. I never even checked."

His reaction seemed genuine, as if this one mistake was going to haunt him for a long time. Then he seemed to release a breath he'd been holding. "Wait. She kept a second pen in her luggage. Right on top. She knew those pens could save her life, and she made sure to always have two available. He hurried over to the luggage, almost as if he thought he could still save her if he found the pen in time. He pulled out the largest piece of luggage and pushed on the latch. "It's still locked." The same ghostly skin tone washed over him as he fished in his pants pocket. He pulled out a small set of keys. "I had the key with me." The poor man looked close to throwing up.

There was a knock on the bedroom door. A man in a white lab coat stuck his head inside. "I've brought the van, Briggs. But I think you'd better come down and talk to the hotel manager. He nearly had a stroke when he saw me walk through the lobby in my lab coat."

"Well, Nate, it does have the word coroner emblazoned across the back. It might be a little distracting for the other hotel guests." He looked over at Officer Pritchett. "Melody, can you go out there and calm the manager down. Ask him if there are any service exits, so we can remove the body without going through the lobby." He turned toward Parker. "Mr. Hermann, let's step out into the other room so I can ask you some questions. Then we can assist you if you have any next of kin to notify."

"Kin? Just me. I mean, my mother is her sister, but they haven't spoken in years. I was her only family."

"Then I'm very sorry, Mr. Hermann. I'm sure you are very distressed, so we'll keep the questions brief."

On their way out, Briggs instructed the other officer to collect the coffee cup, creamer and check for other prints in the room.

I listened to Detective Briggs interview Parker Hermann as I moved around the front room and looked and smelled for other clues.

"When was the last time you saw your aunt alive?" Briggs asked.

Parker paused. "We left the fair around three. Aunt Marian had me book her a four o'clock appointment in the hotel salon for a manicure. She'd broken a nail at today's book signing, and she said she couldn't stand to look at her uneven nails. We came back to the hotel and got changed. We were both leaving, so I put her purse in the safe. Still can't believe I forgot to pull out the epi-pen."

The hotel suite was large for two people, and since they'd spent most of the day at the food fair, the place had hardly been touched. Everything still smelled of furniture polish, window cleaner and disinfectant.

"And where did you go while your aunt was at the salon?" Briggs continued.

"I drove back to Port Danby and strolled through the town. I stopped at the antique shop and the bakery. I brought back two souvenir cookies. They are in the refrigerator. I put them in there before I went into the bedroom and found . . ." His voice trailed off.

"You've had a big shock, Mr. Hermann." Briggs was working on his sympathetic tone, but it needed just a little more finesse.

I walked into the kitchen and was about to glance in the refrigerator to check for the cookies when I reminded myself not to touch anything. I took a paper towel and grabbed the bottom of the refrigerator handle, a place where most people wouldn't touch. I pulled the refrigerator open. Parker had been telling the truth. A lighthouse cookie and a Graystone Church cookie sat on the top shelf of the refrigerator. The only other items in the refrigerator were a bottle of white wine, (the expensive kind) and a bottle of Marian's special creamer. The plastic tab was still secured over the top, so it hadn't been opened. I closed the refrigerator, and I crumpled up the paper towel. As I smashed it between my palms, a fragrance floated off of it. Honey lavender hand lotion. Whoever touched the refrigerator had tried Celeste's sample of hand lotion.

I walked out to the front room. Briggs was just putting away his notepad.

"Mr. Hermann," I piped up and drew both men's attention my way. "By any chance, did you sample some of the honey lavender hand lotion that was being distributed at the fair?"

Parker's brows scrunched together. "Why on earth would I do that?" I had apparently insulted his masculinity.

Briggs knew I wasn't asking just because I was curious. He looked at Parker. "So you didn't rub any on your hands."

"Certainly not."

"What about your aunt?" I asked.

"My aunt has coffee creamer flown in from France. Do you honestly think she's the type to try some homespun, country bumpkin hand lotion recipe?" And there was that wonderful streak of charm he had inherited from his aunt.

"No, of course not. I apologize." I had to work hard to remain polite because the man's aunt and seemingly only family member had just been found dead on a hotel bed.

A quiet exit had been arranged for the removal of the late Marian Fitch from her hotel room. Parker stood nearby, wringing his hands and looking properly distressed as the coroner rolled the gurney through. Detective Briggs and I waited in the hallway to make sure the coast was clear, so they could take her through to the service elevator and out the back through the hotel loading dock.

"The lavender hand lotion?" Briggs asked as we waited for them to roll Marian out of the room.

"I used a napkin to look inside the refrigerator. The cookies were there, by the way. And another bottle of the creamer. But as I crumpled up the napkin, I smelled the hand lotion. It's very strong stuff. I could hardly taste my spicy sweet potato fries over the smell of it on my hands."

"So someone had it on their hands, and they touched the handle of the refrigerator."

"Seems that way."

The gurney rolled toward us. Marian's hand was the only visible part beneath the white sheet.

"Hold it for just a second," Briggs said. "This is your last chance to see if there's any hint of lavender."

"Right. I suppose I should, just in case." Marian's nails had just been freshly painted in a dark pink color. "She had a manicure so it wouldn't be on her hands anymore, and it would be hard to smell over the strong lacquer smell of nail polish." I breathed in deeply along her wrist and sleeve. "I don't smell any lavender."

"Thanks." He waved the coroner on, and they rolled Marian toward the service elevator.

CHAPTER 14

Detective Briggs and I headed back into the hotel room. He had some details to discuss with the Mayfield police, and he'd asked me to sniff around for more of the lavender smell. If neither Parker nor Marian had tried the lotion, that meant someone else had been in the room.

I'd gone over most of the front room and bathroom by the time Briggs had wrapped up with his team. They were still in the bedroom discussing the matter. I noticed that Officer Pritchett fell instantly silent as I walked in.

"Carry on," I said. "Don't mind me." I tapped my nose. "Just doing my bloodhound impression."

From the corner of my eye, I caught Briggs suppressing a smile. It was hard not to be terribly fond of a man who understood my *unique* sense of humor.

"See if there's any lavender fragrance on the phone, Miss Pinkerton," Briggs called from the group. "And remember not to touch it."

I shot him a *seriously* look and walked over to the phone. It had not been placed properly on the charging stand. It was more than possible that Marian had tried to call for help but was already struggling to breathe too much to talk. The poor woman must have been terrified.

I lowered my face to the phone but found no lavender smell. I continued on through the room and walked past a trash can that was empty except for a tissue. The tissue looked as if it hadn't been used. I lowered my face to the can, and there it was. Celeste's lavender and honey hand lotion.

"Detective Briggs, the tissue in this trash can has some traces of the hand lotion on it. But there isn't any on the phone."

Briggs walked over and stared into the can. "It looks like a fresh tissue. Whoever grabbed the handle of the refrigerator suddenly wised up about touching things in the room. They might have used the tissue to pick up the phone and order a free coffee." He motioned for me to follow. "Pritchett, make sure this tissue is added to the evidence collection. Miss Pinkerton and I are going down to the hotel kitchen to see who took the coffee order from this suite. I think if we get that answer, we'll find out who tampered with the creamer."

Briggs and I walked out into the hallway. The lights were on for the guest elevator. "It looks like the main elevators are working again." I pushed the button, and seconds later, the familiar ding sounded, letting us know the elevator had arrived.

We stepped inside. "So you think it'll be as simple as figuring out who called from the room for coffee?" I asked. "But what if it was Marian herself? I mean, it makes sense."

"Yes, except she was at a four o'clock manicure appointment. It's entirely possible she called just before walking down to her appointment. We'll have to fill in the timeline by asking some of the employees."

"Yes, *we* will."

We stepped inside the elevator, and he pushed G for ground floor. "There you go again getting excited about my use of the word *we*."

I walked to the back wall and leaned against it. Briggs joined me. "I didn't say a word," I insisted.

"Well, the truth is, it would've taken us longer to find out the cause of death if you hadn't smelled peanut butter. This would still just be an unexplained death and not a homicide."

"So you've ruled out accidental?" Just as I asked the question, the elevator came to an abrupt halt. The lights flickered off and on and went off completely, bathing us in the pitch dark.

"Oh!" I gasped as I turned toward the tall silhouette standing next to me. I clutched his shirt. His hand felt warm and protective on my arm.

The lights turned on. With some effort, the elevator started up again. The instant change from dark to light caught me by surprise. I was still clutching the fabric of his shirt. He lowered his hand from my arm. The tilt of his mouth assured me, he'd found the entire event amusing.

I released his shirt and smoothed my palm over the ruffled fabric. "Sorry, I get a little panicked in the dark. It's this thing I have—" I shook my head. "Anyhow." I took a steadying breath. He watched me, still wearing a hint of a grin.

I leaned back against the wall of the elevator and stared straight ahead. Me and my stupid fear of the dark.

Thankfully, the doors opened and the fresh air of the ground floor rushed in to cool my warm cheeks. I couldn't tell if the blush was from embarrassment or because I'd instantly turned into the man's arms. Possibly both.

We walked to the kitchen. The usual loud voices, clamor of pots and pans and sounds of food sizzling thrummed behind the two swinging doors.

Detective Briggs pulled out his badge to get us into the 'employees only' entrance. A nice young woman with a tilted cook's hat and over-sized white coat led us to the room service station.

We were greeted by a woman wearing a badge that said 'room service manager'. Her name was Connie. Detective Briggs showed her his badge and introduced me as Miss Pinkerton.

"I was wondering if you kept a log of room service calls. In partic-ular, a log for the free coffee service?"

"Oh yes. I've already pulled it out, assuming you'd want to see it. Mr. Trumble called down here to fill me in on some things," she added quickly. "Terrible tragedy." She reached for a clipboard on her desk. "This was this afternoon's log for the free coffee service. It will tell you what time the call came in, the room number, the order and the name of the server who delivered it."

I peered over Briggs' shoulder as he ran his finger down the list. "Room 801 called at 4:03 and ordered one house specialty coffee, black. It was delivered at five by someone named Neil." Briggs looked up from the clipboard. "Is it possible to talk to Neil and to the person who took the order?"

"Yes, certainly," Connie said. "Neil should be back in a moment. He was just delivering an order. But I'm afraid you won't be able to talk to Vincent. He takes the orders for the coffee service. He's left for the weekend. He and his friends go"—she held up air quotes—"off the grid camping. No technology. Just mother nature." A short dry laugh followed. "I suppose I shouldn't be so sarcastic. I wish my teenagers would consider a weekend off the grid. A day or even an hour off the grid would be wonderful."

"When will Vincent be back?" Briggs asked.

"Not until Monday morning." She looked past us. "Here's Neil. Neil, could you come here for just a moment. Detective Briggs and his assistant would like to ask you about the delivery up to Room 801."

Neil had the bottom half of his hair shaved and the top half was left long. He had it combed to one side, but it hung in his eyes some. He looked a little nervous at first when Connie mentioned the word detective but then he seemed to understand what it was about.

"Yeah?" he asked.

Briggs pulled out his notepad and asked his full name, which was Neil Plummer. "You delivered a free house specialty coffee up to Room 801 at five o'clock."

"That's the woman who died, huh? That grumpy lady with the black hair and face powder." Neil held up his hands. "Wasn't me. I didn't even know the lady. Even though she didn't give me a tip, I didn't kill her."

"Oh, Neil," Connie interjected. "Don't be ridiculous. Just answer the questions."

Briggs nodded a thank you toward Connie. "Was there anyone else in the room with her?"

It had only been a few hours ago, but it seemed Neil had to do quite a memory search to remember. Of course, he had probably been to a lot of rooms today. "Nah, she was alone. Unless someone was in the back rooms, but I didn't see anyone else."

"So she took the coffee and didn't tip you. Anything else?"

"Well, yeah." He flipped aside the long strands of hair that had dropped over his eyes. "She didn't really want the coffee. She said she hadn't even ordered it. In fact, at first she told me to take it back to the kitchen. I turned to leave, and she called me back. She said, 'on second thought, I could use it'. I handed her the coffee, waited politely for a tip, but the only thing I got was the door slammed in my face."

Briggs looked surprised by the last statement.

I leaned my head closer and spoke quietly. "Totally in character with the woman I met at the fair."

Briggs nodded. "Right. Thank you, Neil. You've been helpful. There might be a few more questions at another time." He turned to Connie. "And I'll still need to talk to Vincent when he plugs back into the grid."

CHAPTER 15

*T*he sun had set on the long, extremely eventful day. I wasn't sure what would happen in the morning with the fair. Visitors had come to town, rented rooms and even flown from other states for a three day event. Many of the participants had spent good money and driven miles with their wares to be part of it all. It didn't seem right to shut the entire thing down early, but then it seemed disrespectful to continue on with a jovial, happy event when a woman had died in an apparent homicide. Which also left the question of whether or not one of the fair participants had had their hand in her peanut oil poisoning. I didn't envy Detective Briggs' position. It seemed he needed to get down to a serious suspect before everyone packed up and went home. He told me that he couldn't insist anyone stay in town unless he had some firm evidence to keep them there.

Briggs had dropped me at my shop. Fortunately, I'd driven my car into town instead of my bicycle. There had been just a little too much traffic on the roads for my comfort level, and I'd decided I was safer driving to work. The only shop lights still on were my own and Lola's office light.

Mayfield was a close neighbor of Port Danby. Many people had family living in one of the two towns. I was sure news of Marian

Fitch's death had already reached Port Danby. Especially because Fitch seemed to be the big name and most famous blogger at the fair.

Kingston glowered at me with sleepy eyes from his perch. It was equally good that I'd brought my car. My bird would stop being cranky about being left alone so long once he realized he was getting a ride in the car, something he loved almost more than his sunflower seeds.

"I just need a few minutes, Kingston, and then I promise a fun ride home in the car." I stroked his head and tossed some shelled peanuts into his dish. I watched him picked up a peanut in his beak and wondered if Marian Fitch had been open about her allergy. I decided to take a quick browse through her website before shutting down my computer.

I was heading to my office space when I heard a knock on the front window.

Lola's face peered through the glass. I hurried to let her inside.

"Is it true? That grumpy lady with the Sugar Lips is dead?"

"She didn't actually have sugar lips but yes. She is dead."

"I knew it. The rumors started buzzing through town, but I think Yolanda was trying to squelch them. Everything had been going so perfectly. This sure throws a wrench into things, eh? Come to the Port Danby Food Fair. Only you might never leave."

As inappropriate as it was, it was hard not to respond with a smile. "You are tired, Lola. You should head home."

"I am but I figured you'd have some of the details."

"Why is that?"

"Because I saw you being dropped off by Detective Briggs." She added in a little eye roll for good measure. "And, of course, it was all business. He needed your nose for snooping evidence."

"As a matter of fact that is exactly right."

"What happened? Do they know? Did she just drop dead out of meanness, or did someone take her out?"

When Lola was tired her mood could go in one of two directions, namely, grumpy or kooky. The latter seemed to be the case this evening.

"It might have been foul play."

She pointed at me. "I knew it. I could see it in your face. It's that nephew. He couldn't take all those years of being insulted and pushed around by his overbearing aunt. And then there's what I heard him saying today."

Being tired myself, I had only been half listening to what she was saying, but now she had my full attention. "When did you hear him and what did he say?"

Lola beamed, thrilled to have something important to tell me. "Parker walked in with a woman, a pretty girl with tawny curls. Not one of the bloggers. A visitor, I think. He seemed excited to have met someone, and he was doing the usual bragging and rooster strutting that guys do when you first start dating them and they want to impress you. The woman was admiring an expensive antique diamond bracelet in the glass case, and Parker was bragging about how he was the sole heir to his aunt's fortune. He said it was the only reason he stuck it out with the 'old hag.'" Lola paused. "His words, not mine. Sounds like a good motive, right?" She followed her narrative with a long yawn.

"Yes, it does, and it sounds like a good stopping point for now. Go home and get some sleep. I'm right behind you after I finish up something in the office."

Lola trudged heavy footed to the door. "I am feeling the effects of the long day in my bones. I'm too young to feel this old." She reached the door. "I'll see you tomorrow." She stopped before walking out and looked back at me. "Do you think the fair will continue?"

"Good question. Good night, Lola."

"Good night." She walked out.

I slipped into my tiny office and sat at the computer. Marian had handed me her business card, and I'd dropped it on the desk with the mail. My fingers dashed around the keyboard, and I pulled up her blog. It was a nice, professionally designed site, complete with blog posts and recipes. She actually managed to sound charming and personable in her posts as I skimmed through a few. Maybe someone else was writing them? Or maybe she was just more likable from behind a keyboard than face to face.

I stifled my own yawn and decided to skim blog post titles for anything pertinent. As she'd mentioned, she had a post about her wonderful coffee creamer. (Ironically, the wonderful creamer that'd caused her death.) She waxed poetically about the silky smoothness and the vanilla essence of the creamer and how she wouldn't drink a drop of coffee without it. Then, in a snooty twist, she mentions that it's quite costly and has to be flown in from France.

I skimmed down along the comments where it was easy to see the usual fan club responses of how wonderful the creamer sounds and so on, but one comment stood out, partially due to the font being used and also from the negative response. The commenter went by the name 'SourGrapes' and they used an italic bold font. It seemed unusual to see someone writing in italic bold font.

The comment was pretty harsh. *'Do you actually think anyone cares what kind of coffee creamer you use, you fake charlatan? You're a fake and everyone knows it.'*

I scrolled down. A few people came to Marian's defense, but most people ignored the comment. I glanced at the topics on Marian's other posts. There were several about her deadly peanut allergy. This meant people who visited her blog knew she had it. It was no secret. That certainly put a different light on things.

CHAPTER 16

$\mathcal{W}$ hen I worked in the big city, a rainstorm meant wet overcoats, frizzy hair and the constant search for a place to park my umbrella. It meant standing under the thin eaves of the bus stop and avoiding ankle deep puddles that would instantly turn expensive shoes into worthless dog chew toys. In other words, rain, wind and thunder in the city meant major inconvenience in every way. But in my new, quaint small town of Port Danby, a rainstorm meant spectacular night time light shows, the melodic drumming of raindrops on the roof and hot berry tea on the sofa with my cat curled up next to me purring along with the beat of the rain.

By the time Kingston and I had pulled up in the driveway of my cozy house, the drops had begun to tip toe lightly on the windshield and cement walkway. An hour later, after I'd filled my empty belly with hot tomato soup and crackers, the rain had started to fall, less in drops, and more in sheets.

I sipped my tea and stared out at the night sky. An occasional streak of lightning would illuminate the gray pillows of moisture drifting through the dark sky. Thunder rumbled in the distance, somewhere out on the water. The weatherman had forecast a possible rainstorm, so most of the bloggers had taken precautions with their equipment and supplies. With this latest unexpected turn of events, I doubted if it mattered now. It seemed quite possible that the fair would shut down early.

Detective Briggs would have to move his investigation along at full speed. When Kingston and I drove away from the shop, I saw his car still parked in front of the police station. It wasn't surprising to see him working late.

I carried my teacup into the kitchen and lifted the sheer curtains to glance next door. A flickering light told me Dash was watching television in the front room. I hadn't seen him since the dance, but then he was always busy working on boats at the marina. And when he wasn't fixing boats, he was working on his house. And, I had no doubt that in between he was going on dates. He had been a veritable rock star at the dance. Just as I'd predicted.

Before I sat back down on the couch, I picked up the pictures I'd *borrowed* from the Hawksworth gardening shed. The day had been so busy, I'd forgotten to return them. I decided to look through them, so I could return the pictures first thing in the morning.

Typical Lacey, I thought. It was a perfectly snuggly night, in my perfectly snuggly house, on my perfectly snuggly couch with my snuggle loving cat, and I was pulling out century old murder scene photos. I put on my reading glasses, deciding that I would need them to see the details clearly in the faded photos.

Photographs at the turn of the century tended to have an ethereal dreamscape or in many cases a nightmare-scape quality. Photographers at the time didn't know the phrase 'say cheese', and virtually no one smiled in a portrait. Even children looked stone-faced, and the staged lighting gave everyone a slightly crazed stare. I'd read several theories on the somber faced pictures. One theory proposed that dental hygiene was so bad back then people weren't apt to show off their teeth. A second more plausible theory was that it was considered more dignified not to smile and that unprompted grinning was for the lewd and lower class. If grim, serious expressions were considered the height of good taste, then the Hawksworth family had reached a lofty status indeed. The three children sat in various positions around an upholstered settee while the parents sat in the middle. Everyone was staring directly at the camera as if they had been hypnotized by the lens. I turned the picture over. Someone, probably Mrs. Hawksworth, had written their names and October 1901 on the back in pencil.

There was one more family portrait where Mr. Hawksworth was sporting thick mutton chops, and Mrs. Hawksworth had a tight little bun on top her head, making both her head and shoulders, in puffed sleeves, look bigger than average. The room was decorated for the Christmas holiday. Sprigs of evergreens had been hung on the ornate mantel behind them and a tinsel covered tree sat in the corner of the room. The date on the back said December 1905. It was a photo of their last holiday. The final picture, the one I'd saved for last, was the crime scene photograph. While family portraits were staged and probably took hours to pull off, the police photographer had taken much less care for his gruesome subject matter.

The storm outside had churned into an angry wind that spit rain against my front window. The room lit up bright white and a loud clap of thunder followed, causing Nevermore to lift his head, but only for a second.

I sat forward and moved the picture closer to the lamp on the end table. Mrs. Hawksworth was splayed out on her stomach. The dark edges of what I could only surmise was a pool of blood spread out past the voluminous layers of her dress. Just ten feet away, Mr. Hawksworth was curled on his side. The photo was taken to show the back of his head, or what was left of it. And sitting just below his limp right hand was a handgun. A smear of blood stretched out behind him, which seemed odd. If the man had shot himself in the head, he would not have been writhing in pain on the ground before succumbing to the head wound. His damaged skull seemed to indicate that death was instant.

A wind gust howled around my house, and the lights flickered for a moment. I decided I'd had enough of looking at dead bodies for the day. I put down the pictures and got up to grab some candles just in case of an outage. I only took one step before the lights flashed bright. A loud popping sound followed, then my house went dark. Very dark.

My heart rate sped up, keeping rhythm with the rush of rain on the roof. I glanced toward the front window. The power had gone out all over the town. With no light of any kind outside, I could hardly even see shadows or the outline of furniture.

I moved slowly and felt for the coffee table. I managed to make it past the end of the couch, but without the furniture for my guide, walking across the open floor felt endless and extra scary.

A noise outside on the porch sent Nevermore off the couch and down the hall. If only I had the cat's night vision. Another loud thump outside made the breath stick in my lungs. I turned and looked toward the door. A shadow passed by the window. I was too terrified to scream. I looked around for my phone but couldn't remember where I'd placed it. I stood frozen like a terrified deer in headlights, only there were no headlights.

A loud knock rattled the door, and the scream that had been stuck in my throat shot out.

"Lacey! Are you all right?"

"Dash." I was so relieved to hear his voice, I nearly sobbed his name.

He shined a flashlight through the front window, lighting up my path to the front door.

I pulled it open and had to keep myself from crumpling into a tearful mess. "Dash, I'm so glad to see you. I was just getting up to find candles and—"

As I spoke, bright headlights turned the corner and then lit up my house as the car turned into the driveway. Even in the rain and wind, I recognized that it was Detective Briggs' car. Seconds later, his car backed out and he drove off.

Dash looked at me in question.

I shrugged. "Maybe he was just making the rounds to see that everything in town was all right."

"Yes, only he stopped at your house and decided to skip the rest of the street."

"It's possible. If you can lead me into my kitchen, I can get some candles. And I will be forever grateful."

"Absolutely." He pointed the flashlight into the house as the lights turned back on.

My heart rate and ragged breathing slowed back to normal. Dash was soaked from head to toe.

"I really appreciate you coming to check on me, Dash."

"Well, I know how you feel about the dark. I didn't see any candles or flashlights through your windows, so I thought you could use some assistance."

"Thank you so much. I won't keep you then since you are soaked to the bone."

Dash nodded. "Good night, Lacey."

"Good night."

CHAPTER 17

The evening's rainstorm was long gone, and a dewy moisture evaporated off the buildings and sidewalks as I pedaled along Harbor Lane. I was in need of some fresh air and exercise, so I decided to risk the traffic and ride my bicycle. Kingston flew on ahead. I warned him not to take a detour to the town square, but something told me he'd be ignoring that warning.

I'd expected a relatively quiet morning but discovered a line in front of the shop as I rolled up. And the line wasn't for free cinnamon rolls at the bakery. Most of the faces looked unfamiliar and many had red noses as if they'd been crying. They were Marian's fans, the people who had traveled to Port Danby to meet the owner of Sugar Lips. Some even clutched a copy of her cookbook close to their heart as if it had been some life changing book rather than a collection of recipes.

I looked around but didn't see my crow, which was just as well. Many of the people in line looked as if their nerves were on edge about the tragic news. They might not appreciate a black crow, a bird that was usually a harbinger of doom and death in movies and books.

"Good morning," I said politely as I shimmied my way through the line.

"Are you Pink?" a woman with red eyes and a nose to match asked. "We were told we could buy flowers here for the memorial."

"I am Pink and yes, I do have flowers for sale. What memorial?"

Another woman who didn't have the red puffiness that went along with a good cry but who held tightly to a handkerchief anyhow, stepped briskly forward after quickly appointing herself spokesperson. "I don't know if you've heard about the terrible tragedy, but Marian Fitch is dead."

"Oh yes. I did hear. It's very sad."

"Apparently, the other bloggers are keeping the fair open in her honor," the woman said. "So we're going to turn the Sugar Lips booth into a shrine of sorts by covering it with flowers."

Somehow I was sure that Fitch's honor wasn't the motive behind keeping the fair open, but what did I know? "That is truly lovely of all of you." I opened up the shop. "Step inside then, and we'll see which flowers will suit Marian's memorial."

Less than one hour after Marian's loyal and bereft fans swept through Pink's Flowers, the store was empty of customers and of most of the cut flowers. Kingston had waited patiently on the roof until the last customer left before tapping at the front window to come inside. He'd immediately fallen fast asleep on his perch.

I walked into the office to put in an emergency order for more carnations, roses and Gerbera daisies but the clang of the goat bell on the door drew me back out to the store front.

Elsie walked inside carrying a plate of cookies. "My cherry, chocolate and pistachio biscotti. I thought you could use a pick me up after that morning rush."

"Elsie, let me just tell you, that as you walked across my shop floor with those biscotti, I was sure I saw a glowing yellow halo around your head. Which would be fitting, since you are a saint." I picked up the biscotti and took a bite. The earthy crunch of pistachio nuts was offset perfectly by the rich bits of semi-sweet chocolate and the tart dried cherries. "Hmm, as usual, my friend, culinary perfection."

"I'm glad I could provide some bliss." Elsie hopped up on the chair like a fit woman of twenty, even though she was in her sixties. "So how about that? Chaos came after all. Sure didn't expect the fair to be interrupted by a murder."

My face popped up. "How did you already know it was murder?"

Her face lit up. "Ah ha. See, I knew it was murder. Or at least I thought it was until I saw your reaction just now."

I held up the crescent shaped cookie. "I guess it was the old 'feed her biscotti and she'll talk trick'."

"The oldest trick in the book," Elsie said confidently. "I'm not surprised that Marian finally pushed someone to the brink. She's always had plenty of enemies. Even though I never finished the pastry course with her, I left there thinking I never wanted to cross paths with the woman in the business world." Elsie swept up some of the greenery and baby's breath clippings that cluttered my work island. I hadn't had time to tidy up after the mad rush of customers.

"It does seem that someone wanted her dead. And they succeeded." Talking to Elsie reminded me of the brief conversation I'd had with Lola the night before. I needed to let Detective Briggs know about Parker being the heir to her fortune. Money and fortune was always an iron clad motive. And her nephew had, conveniently enough, put both epinephrine pens out of her reach by having them locked up. Of course I knew that Briggs was already working hard on the case. And I was sure he was looking extra hard at Parker. They always looked at family members first as suspects.

"You know, there was something about a cookbook deal a few years back," Elsie began. She tapped her chin as she tried to summon the details from her memory. "Marian's cookbook was sold in auction to some big publishing house. It knocked another prominent blogger's cookbook out of the running. But gosh darn, I can't remember any more than that. You know I spent a little time with a baking blog, Elsie's Sweets," she continued. "That was the name of the blog, but I discovered that opening an actual bakery made a heck of a lot more money than a virtual bakery. I gave up on it fast, but I did frequent some of the same sites as the other bloggers. That's how I heard about Marian's book deal. But any negative press about the deal was cleaned up right afterward. Marian always had a great public relations firm keeping her image charming and innocent. Even though she was neither." Elsie's phone timer rang. She had it set to Beethoven's Fifth so it couldn't be ignored. "I've got more biscotti ready to come out of the oven." She hopped off the chair. "I am sort of surprised that they decided to continue the fair. I'm sure Yolanda did a good deal of tossing and turning last night, trying to decide what to do. Poor thing, it had all been going so smoothly."

"Marian's fans told me the other bloggers decided to continue in honor of Marian Fitch."

Elsie smiled. "Yes, I'll believe that when I look in the mirror and see a real halo over my head. I'll see you later, Pink. Enjoy the biscotti."

CHAPTER 18

*E*lsie's biscotti had gotten me through the morning, but my stomach was grumbling for something heartier. The day had started like a whirlwind, but things had calmed down enough for me to take a stroll down to the fair. After getting something to eat, I planned to circle back to the police station to see if I could catch Briggs in his office. I was going to mention the few details I'd discovered from Lola and Elsie, hoping they would help. Although, none of it seemed like much.

I was almost a little disappointed that Briggs hadn't stopped by to fill me in on how things were going with the case. I was, after all, the person to discover the crucial detail—the peanut butter in the creamer. I decided to blame it on Briggs being too busy to stop by.

I crossed the street and poked my head into Lola's shop, thinking I'd invite her along for some lunch, but she was busy with customers. The fair had certainly brought a lot of business to the shops in town. Lola waved and smiled but continued with her sales pitch. I'd bring her back a sandwich or some chicken wings.

I headed down Harbor Lane and was disappointed to see that Detective Briggs' car was not parked out front. As I rounded the corner on Pickford Way, I was surprised to see several large white vans with satellite equipment on top. Each one of the northern corners of the square was cluttered with news crews, cameras and reporters. Some of the visitors and bloggers were being interviewed.

I reached the town square. Many of the visitors were snapping pictures of the Sugar Lips booth that was now blooming with Pink's Flowers. The visitors might have been distraught by the loss of their favorite food blogger, but the other fair participants didn't look the slightest bit distressed by her death.

One person who did look entirely distressed was Yolanda. She was standing in front of the vegan booth sucking down a thick green smoothie through a straw. But it wasn't a happy straw suck. Her cheeks collapsed into two sharp cheek bones with each draw. Her eyes were darting back and forth between news crews.

It took her a moment to notice me as I walked up. Yolanda released her death grip on the straw. An audible swallow was followed by a deep, steadying breath. "I needed this. I haven't eaten all day. Oh, Lacey, I don't know what to think. Mayor Price won't even come out of his office. He is so upset that Port Danby is now going to be associated with a murder."

"Yolanda, you know Mayor Price is always a glass half empty type. You are the glass half full type. This fair has brought tons of business to the shops. I just had my best morning ever. Of course, that was due mainly to the murder, but still, there's always a bright side when you look for it."

"Good advice, Lacey. I'll try and remember that. In the meantime, I hope these news crews clear out of here soon." Something else caught her eye past my shoulder. She took another big gulp of smoothie. "I know he's just doing his job, but I sure wish Detective Briggs wasn't hanging around asking people questions. It puts such a negative spin on the whole thing."

I followed the direction of her gaze and spotted Detective Briggs standing between the cream puffs and submarine sandwiches. He had out his notebook, and he was writing down details.

"Uh, Yolanda, I'm pretty sure the negative spin happened when Marian Fitch was found dead in her hotel room. Detective Briggs has a tough job. He has to find a solid suspect before everyone packs up and leaves town."

"I suppose you're right. I just wish he wouldn't make it look so official. But I suppose that comes with the job too."

"It does. And I've got a few things to tell him, so I'll see you later, Yolanda. And try not to worry about Mayor Price. He'll come around." I added the last note, even though I didn't necessarily believe it. I'd only ever known him to be a grump.

Briggs was hastily writing something down. His eyes lifted more than once when he spotted me walking toward him. He kept his expression solid and serious as his pen scrawled over the notepad. The woman he'd been talking to, the cream puff baker, walked away leaving him alone to finish up what he was writing.

"Didn't expect to see you here," I said cheerily.

"I'm investigating a murder that's connected to this food fair. Where else would I be?" The chill in his tone was something I'd never heard before, and I hoped I would never hear it again.

His cold greeting had left me a little hurt and totally speechless. He sensed my discomfort, but it seemed to take a great deal of effort for him to look at me. "I'm sorry, Miss Pinkerton. It's just I'm very busy. I need to interview a few people, especially since most will be leaving town in two days." With that semi apology he headed away.

I stood and watched him, feeling perplexed, stunned and sad. Then it occurred to me that I'd done nothing at all to deserve it. I'd helped him figure out Marian's cause of death. Otherwise, they'd still be waiting for the coroner's report just to see if it was murder.

I hurried to catch up to him. "I have some information, but maybe you've decided I'm no longer useful to the investigation. In which case, I'll just walk boldly away."

He didn't answer, but I caught just a slight shift of his jaw, which meant he was thinking about saying something. But no words followed.

"Fine, I'm leaving." I swung my arms at my sides and took long steps. I peeked back at him over my shoulder. He was watching me. "This is my walking boldly away look. Do you think it works?"

An edge of a smile appeared but that was all he allowed. "What is your information, Miss Pinkerton?"

I nearly skipped back to him. "Two things. Lola overheard Parker Hermann bragging to some girl that he was going to inherit his aunt's fortune when she died. This was before she died, of course." I thought for a second. "Actually, in a pinch of irony, I think he was in Lola's store bragging to the girl at the time that his aunt . . . Well, you get the picture. Also, Elsie went to pastry school with Marian and some of the other bloggers. She said a few years ago another blogger lost out on a big publisher offer for her cookbook because Marian swooped in and got the deal."

Briggs had taken out his notebook and was writing down my information. I got temporarily distracted by how long his dark lashes were as he looked down.

He realized I'd stopped talking and glanced up. Those long lashes were the perfect frame for his dark eyes. "Did Elsie say who the blogger was? Was it the same blogger who had her donut recipe stolen?"

I snapped out of my short trance. "Twyla? I don't know. Elsie couldn't remember who lost the cookbook deal. And apparently Marian's PR person took care of any lingering dirty laundry surrounding it. This happened awhile ago though, so I'm sure that tidbit of information is useless."

"At the moment, the nephew is my top suspect."

"But he was at Lola's and Elsie's at the time of Marian's death."

"Exactly. Conveniently absent with the luggage keys in his pocket. The creamer had been tampered with before the coffee came. Hermann could have added in the peanut butter and gone off to town."

"Right. Of course. Makes sense."

"Well, I've got more interviews to do. I'll let you get back to your day." He'd reverted back to being standoffish, as if we were just casual acquaintances. I felt the disappointment deep down in my chest.

"Oh, all right. That's fine."

He began to walk away, but I decided to bring up the night before. "I was sure I saw you pull into my driveway last night."

Briggs stopped and stared at his notepad as if he was looking for an explanation on the paper. "Just thought I'd check on you. The power was out, and after the elevator incident, I discovered you weren't fond of the dark."

"Thank you. You should have stopped in." I was reading so many signals from him I wasn't sure what to think.

He shook his head. "I saw you were already being looked after." There was that chilled tone again. "Good day, Miss Pinkerton."

I blinked back an ache in my eyes as I watched him walk away.

CHAPTER 19

My y unpleasant few minutes with Detective Briggs had put me through a series of emotions beginning with flabbergasted and ending with exasperated, with a touch of heavy heart in between. He had moved on to the opposite end of the fair. Briggs might have upset me, but that didn't mean I should starve myself. I decided to give one of the Sandwich Queen's treats a try.

The Sandwich Queen had gone off to shop in town, leaving behind two young girls who were eager to help and to let me know which sandwiches were, in their opinion, the best. In the end I decided to try a triple grilled cheese with tomato and pickles. As I waited for my sandwich to come out of the grilled cheese press, I noticed Mayor Price walking, or rather, marching across the street from his office building. His signature puffy moustache rocked back and forth like a boat on a rough sea and his cheeks were dark pink with anger.

I searched around but didn't see Yolanda. The news crews had packed up their equipment, but they lingered around the news vans, possibly just waiting for their next destination order. I didn't know enough about news crews to hazard a guess. But the story here, was, thus far, fairly uneventful. I wouldn't expect them to stay long in Port

Danby. And with the sour lemon twist on the mayor's face, for Yolanda's sake, I hoped they'd drive off soon.

"Here you go," said the spunky girl with a spray of freckles across her nose that reminded me of my own freckled nose.

"Looks yummy. Thanks." I searched around for a place to sit, but most of the tables were taken. The murder hadn't slowed people's cravings for delicious treats.

I headed across the path to a patch of shade. I took a big bite and with it being a triple grilled cheese, the bite was still attached to the sandwich by a mozzarella cheese umbilical cord. I was using my chin and my fingers to un-attach myself when the mayor spurted my name behind me. (Spurting was the best verb I could come up with to describe the way Mayor Price said my name.)

"Miss Pinkerton."

I turned slowly around, having just been victorious in freeing my bite from the sandwich. I quickly chewed and swallowed. "Yes, Mayor Price?"

He pointed up to the top of an ash tree. "Is that your crow?" The mayor truly had a bee in his bonnet about my pet.

I squinted up to the tree. The top branches were moving, but there was no breeze. Some magenta colored leaves fluttered down. The crow on the top branch was surveying the goody filled scene below.

"No, Mayor Price, that's not my crow."

Several yards away at the Sweet Cherry Pie booth, Celeste Bower was flailing her arms and yelling 'go away'. Her hens had chimed in on the frenetic energy in the booth. Chicken feathers filled the air like in a slumber party pillow fight. And at the center of the melee was none other than my pet.

"*That* is my crow." I hurried over to Celeste's booth. Her eyes were wide with terror and rightfully so. Apparently some of the stale flax seed Celeste threw out had missed the trash. Kingston was desperately trying to nibble up the spilled seed.

"Kingston," I said sharply. He was quite focused on the discarded flax.

Celeste was confused that I was calling a wild crow by name. Her brows furrowed together, and her baby blue eyes looked a lot less friendly. Her big country smile had vanished too.

"Is this your bird?" she asked angrily. "A pet crow? He's a menace." She lifted her foot to give Kingston a kick. I was shocked by her display of temper after acting the charismatic country charmer all weekend.

"No, please. He's just a little too comfortable around people." I leaned over the side of the booth and lowered my hand to get Kingston's attention. It was a gesture I did when I wanted him to step onto my hand and use my wrist as a perch. He stopped pecking at the grass and hopped onto my arm. I straightened away from the booth, crow on hand and discovered that a curious audience had gathered.

"Look, that crow is tame," I heard someone say.

"I wish I had a pet crow," another voice said.

Most people saw a tame crow as an oddity but a fun oddity. That was not the case with everyone. The only person who looked more angry than Celeste was my dear nemesis, Mayor Price.

"Now you've done it, you daft bird," I muttered to Kingston. He took that as his cue to leave and lifted off my wrist. The crowd pointed up in awe as if they had never seen a crow fly overhead and watched until Kingston was just a black speck in the blue sky.

"Where's he going?" a girl asked.

"If he knows what's good for him—home," I answered. I turned to apologize to Celeste, but the mayor stopped me.

"Miss Pinkerton." The way he said my name caused my shoulders to bunch up around my ears.

"That bird is dangerous. I'm looking into having the council write up legislation to ban crows from the shopping and business areas."

"Someone better tell the other crows then." The deep, smooth voice came through the crowd. Faces turned back to Detective Briggs. He took a sip of the soda he was holding before motioning toward six crows snooping around the tables and trash cans. Even after seeing its comrade nearly get kicked, one crow was still trying desperately to get to the dispersed flax seed. That stuff must have been like crow candy.

With all the ruffled feathers, both human and bird, there was always one person who never had a feather out of place. Detective James Briggs. And the sound of his voice had made me feel safer and bolder all at once.

I made every attempt to stretch up taller. "Mayor Price, if your city council really has nothing better to do than worry about pet birds, then go right ahead. But until then, Kingston will sit in my shop window. And when he tires of the window, he'll fly around the town and the trees just like the other birds."

Mayor Price's mouth had twisted in a knot. He turned to Briggs. "I wouldn't have expected to see you lollygagging around the fair drinking sodas, Detective, when there's a mur—" He sealed his mouth shut, and his eyes flickered as he searched for a different word. "When there's an important case going on."

"I assure you, Mayor Price, I never lollygag. And I'm here for precisely that reason. I hope you don't mind if I stopped for a soda. I was parched. Now I'm heading back to the office to continue on that *case.*"

For the second time that afternoon, I watched Detective Briggs walk away. Only this time, instead of an ache in my eyes, there was the tiniest little pitter patter inside my chest. I was pretty sure it was my heart sighing dreamily.

CHAPTER 20

I'd told myself a dozen times it was a mistake to go into the police station and see Detective Briggs, and yet, there I was pulling open the heavy glass door. The police station was the least inviting place in the entire town, which was saying a lot because the county morgue was just at the edge of Port Danby, past the church and right before the Mayfield turnoff. Still I had to give Officer Chinmoor and Hilda, the woman who ran dispatch, props for trying. For Halloween they had taped some paper Jack-'o'-lanterns to the front of the chin high dull gray counters. And that gray was the only splash of color in the place. For November, they had tried to add a touch of festiveness by taping up a paper pilgrim and turkey. It seemed they'd used the same pieces of tapes as the pumpkins because I was sure I saw a corner of Jack still stuck to the tape over the pilgrim's tall black hat.

Officer Chinmoor must have been out in the police car because it was not parked out front. Hilda, a retired police woman from the next town of Chesterton, popped her head up and removed her headphones. "Hello, Miss Pinkerton. Are you here to see Detective Briggs?"

"If he has a minute, yes." I didn't have much more to tell him, but I was dying to see what he'd discovered in his interviews at the fair.

"Let me check. How is that magical million dollar nose?" she asked, tapping her own nose at the same time.

"It's still on my face. I'm hoping I can be of assistance in the murder investigation if Detective Briggs needs me."

"I'll just check on him and see if he has time. I know he's working hard today." She knocked on the door and entered.

My entire body froze as it suddenly dawned on me he might just say no to seeing me. I tended to look too positively on everything, and I'd immediately concluded that when he stepped in to take my side against Mayor Price, it signaled we were still friends. But just maybe I'd been wrong.

Hilda walked out. I braced myself for disappointment. Her face didn't give me any clues. "Go on in, Miss Pinkerton."

"Right. Thank you. I will." I walked into Briggs' office, which was perhaps one small step above the front office in terms of color and decor. But then it was a detective's office. My few years in the perfume industry where interior design and posh surroundings were tantamount to success had made me far too judgmental. I needed to work on that.

I felt instantly shy in Briggs' presence. I usually felt so at ease with him, but the blustery greeting at the fair this afternoon had broken my confidence.

He was flipping through his notepad. "Have a seat, Miss Pinkerton."

Naturally, I was trying to gauge whether or not the simple request sounded cold or friendly or indifferent. The last option, I decided. Which could be good or bad.

I sat down and rested my hands quietly in my lap, determined not to show my unease by fidgeting with the hem of my shirt or some other meaningless twitch. I waited for him to finish skimming his notes and noticed there was just enough tension in the air to require cutting with a jaunty little opener.

"Well, Mayor Price is obviously growing fonder of me each day."

The edge of his lip curled up so my opener worked. Sort of.

He finally lifted his face to look at me. "The man thinks anyone not born within fifty miles of Port Danby is a hostile alien from another planet."

"Ah, I see. That explains his warm, fuzzy approach with me." I sat forward, relieved that some of the tension had dissipated. "Did you find anything of worth when you were talking to the people at the town square?"

He nodded and flipped to a few pages of notes. "I discovered that our victim was as much loved as she was hated. Of course the haters chose their words carefully so as not to seem suspect. As the Sandwich Queen noted, and I quote— 'Marian was vile. She was the type of person to step on your toe with her heel and then blame you for having a toe in the first place. But she certainly didn't deserve to die. Very sad. Poor dear.'"

"It seems to me that the food bloggers, the people who have been around her in these kinds of events, see her in a totally different light than the people who read her blog and buy her cookbook," I said. "Which makes sense. A lot of people are very different face to face. Those same people can come off as likable and personable through a keyboard. I visited her blog by the way."

"I did too," he said. "I didn't find much except that she really loves that blasted coffee creamer. That and the fact that she broadcast to everyone that she had a deadly peanut allergy. Of course there was nothing wrong with that, except it makes it that much harder to narrow down the list of suspects." He picked up a pad of paper from under a file folder. "Which, for the time being, is a list of one. Her nephew, Parker Hermann."

"That is a short list. Where is Parker at the moment?"

"At the hotel. He did book another suite though. The crime scene room is locked so no one, not even housekeeping, can enter. He's waiting to fly home with his aunt's remains. I've asked him to stay here until I get a clearer picture of what happened to her. But right now I don't have anything to keep him here indefinitely."

"Nothing else came out of the fair interviews?" I asked.

"Yes, one more thing. Apparently just about every person at the fair tried a sample of that honey-lavender hand lotion. I'm afraid that piece of evidence is worthless."

"That's a shame." I sat for a moment and had a quick mind debate about whether or not to approach him about this afternoon's greeting. I'd come to the conclusion that it had to do with the rainy night and power outage and most of all with my neighbor, Dash.

"Detective Briggs," I said, somewhat hesitantly.

"Yes?"

"I'm just going to say something here. I tend to ramble on when something has me upset, so please excuse me if my words get disjointed."

He sat back and tilted his head just a tad defensively. He must have known the topic I was heading toward.

"I live next door to Dashwood Vanhouten. I didn't know him before I bought and moved into my house. He has been polite and kind and exceedingly attentive. He even stepped in on at least two occasions when I was in trouble."

His brows furrowed in question.

I waved my hand dismissively. "A little incident falling off my porch and then once more when I got stuck inside the . . . Let's just say I got stuck somewhere and leave it at that. My point is—"

"Yes, what is your point?"

This time, I tilted my head defensively. "I'm getting to it. Dash is a friend of mine. He rushed over last night when he knew the power was out. He also knew I'd be distressed by the dark. Not that it's anyone's business, but he is a friend and a neighbor and that's all. You have both made no effort to hide the fact that you two don't care for each other, but whatever that's about has nothing to do with me. I'm not part of that triangle. There is Dash and me, friends and neighbors. And there is Detective Briggs and me, friends—I hope—and investigative partners."

He rubbed the black beard stubble on his jaw. "We're not investigative partners."

I shrugged. "I thought I'd throw that in to give it a whirl and see how it sounded. I rather liked it."

He shook his head and then gazed at me across the desk. "We are friends, Miss Pinkerton. And you're right. Whatever has passed between Dash and me has nothing to do with you. I apologize."

"Apology accepted. And thank you."

"Thank you for what?"

"For stopping by last night to make sure I was all right. Or maybe you were just making the rounds?"

He seemed to contemplate his response. "No, I stopped by to make sure you were all right."

"Then thank you."

His phone rang.

I stood up. "I'll leave you to it then."

He picked up the phone. "Hello. Yes, this is Detective Briggs."

I reached the door.

"Right. Hold on, please. Miss Pinkerton," he called before I walked out.

I turned around.

"The manager, Mr. Trumble, wants his expensive suite back. I need to go in and do one last sweep for evidence. Would you like to go?"

"Yes," I said faster than a blink.

He finished his phone call, hung up and grabbed his keys.

I did a quick little clap of my hands.

"What's the applause for?" he asked as he got up from his desk.

"It's my happy applause. You've never done a happy applause?"

"Can't say I have."

"You should." I followed him out the door.

He stopped before opening the car door. "What about your shop?"

"No problem. I'm out of flowers, anyhow."

CHAPTER 21

The manager looked just as harried as the day of the murder when he came skating on his hard soled leather shoes across the marble floor of the lobby. I wondered if he was just a naturally hyper kind of guy, always looking as if he'd had just one espresso too many.

"Glad you are here, Detective Briggs. As I had Blanche, my assistant manager, mention on the phone, I just can't afford to have that suite vacant for much longer. If the crew could get in there and clean, then—"

"Yes, I understand how the hotel system works, Mr. Trumble," Detective Briggs said. "I would like to make one more thorough check of the room before we hand it over to cleaning crews. If you could let us in or get us a key, that would be great."

"A key. Right." He was just about to scurry off for a key, but Briggs stopped him. "Mr. Trumble, just for clarification, Ms. Fitch did have the room rented for the entire weekend, correct?"

"Yes, they arrived Thursday. Like most of the others."

"Then how are you losing money on the room when the weekend hasn't ended?"

Mr. Trumble scooted closer. "Well, the nephew rented another room. So I just moved the charge to the new room. I didn't feel right charging him for two rooms. He did just lose his aunt, after all."

"Yes, very hospitable of you. One more question." Briggs pulled his notepad out and feathered through it, finally stopping a few pages back. "By any chance, has Vincent returned from his camping trip?"

Mr. Trumble's overly fluffy brows did a quick dance. "Oh yes, Vincent. Of course. I have two hundred employees, you understand. I believe he doesn't return to work until Monday morning. But I can check if anyone has spoken to him. I know he goes off into the wilderness to do whatever it is kids do these days." He winked and shucked Briggs on the arm. "Guess we all did that in our day too, eh?"

I pressed my hand over my lips and turned my head to hide my smile. Briggs elbowed me lightly.

"I imagine our *days* might have been at different times but I'm sure you're right. Some things never change. Now, if you could bring us the key, we'll get on with our work. Then you can have your suite back."

"Of course." He raced off and returned with the key marked 801.

We headed to the elevators. The doors opened. I hesitated for just a second. "I sure hope they got this thing fixed. I don't want another ride like the last one."

"Really?" We stepped inside, and he pushed the button. "I kind of enjoyed it."

I looked over at him. He stared straight ahead, but I caught a little twinkle in his eye.

As we stepped off the elevator, the wheels of a maintenance man's cart squeaked down the hallway. Instead of turning left to the room, Briggs motioned for me to follow him to the right. We turned the corner to follow the cart. The man was dressed in pale blue coveralls. He didn't hear us walk up behind him as he pushed a key into the lock and opened up an apparently vacant room. He smiled and nodded politely at us before dropping the key on the cart, grabbing his tool box and disappearing inside the room.

Detective Briggs stopped at the cart and looked at it.

"What are we doing?" I asked.

"I'm just wondering if the key he so casually just dropped on this cart is specifically for the room or if it's a master key."

Without another thought, Briggs picked up the key and walked to the next room. He knocked once. A woman called out that she didn't need any towels.

Briggs went across the hallway and knocked on another door. No answer. He pushed the key into the lock. It opened. He shut the room door again and made sure it was locked before returning to the cart. He tossed the key back in place just as the maintenance man walked out of the room.

The man eyed us suspiciously as we walked back around the corner. We still didn't go to Fitch's room. Briggs tugged my hand to stop me and pressed his finger against his mouth to let me know to stay quiet. The wheels of the cart squeaked again. We peered around the corner and watched the man perform almost the same ritual of opening a door, dropping the key on the cart and picking up his tool box.

Briggs turned around. "I've seen enough. Let's go to the suite."

"I guess it would be terribly easy to get into any room with the maintenance man's master key sitting on that cart."

"That's exactly what I was thinking."

"Well, great minds and all that," I noted as we headed into Marian Fitch's suite.

"I know Officer Pritchett and her team went through for prints and didn't find much. By the way, the tests showed you were right about her cause of death. The creamer had peanut butter in it."

"Which means the only murder weapon was the infamous coffee creamer. That does make evidence slim. Maybe I'll just send this nose around the room once to see if I turn up anything else."

His laugh was unexpected. "You talk about your nose as if it wasn't attached to your face."

"It does sort of have a mind of its own. Maybe I should consider giving it a name. *This nose* seems kind of informal. I'm going to start in the bedroom."

"That works. I'm heading to the kitchen where the so-called murder weapon was tampered with."

I walked into the bedroom. It was an entirely different room without the dead body draped across the bed. It was hard to believe any crime had taken place in it. And I supposed, in the next few days, new visitors would be sleeping in the same bed. That thought gave me a chill. I wondered if there was any law that made hotels disclose when someone died in a room.

I searched every inch of the room, taking in long deep inhales to pick up all the molecules of scent. Nothing stood out as out of place or wrong. I continued out to the main room and walked over to the seating area where the room's telephone was sitting. I knew they'd already dusted it for prints, but still, I grabbed a tissue from the box on the end table and picked up the phone just to give it a whiff. Nothing but disinfectant. As I put the phone down, I dropped the tissue. I reached down to pick it up from the rug, and as I did, an odor rose up from the plush carpet. Whatever was on the carpet was strong enough to taint the tissue. I dropped down to my knees, took a deep breath and winced at the unpleasant odor.

I glanced up to find Briggs staring down at me over the back of the couch. "Did you find something?"

"I found something, but I don't know if it has anything to do with the case. It is just a strange odor." I leaned down again for another breath and had to swallow back the bitter taste in my throat. "Wow, I'm trying to think of a way to describe it. It's as if someone took a dead fish and dipped it in old paint."

Briggs pulled out his notepad. "May I quote you on that?"

I laughed. "As long as you're the only person reading those notes." I pushed to my feet. "Other than the weird smell that I can't possibly figure the source for, I found nothing. How about you?"

"Nope. Seems like I'm just hitting walls today. Let's head back to Port Danby."

CHAPTER 22

*W*e'd returned to Port Danby in the late afternoon without much more to go on except that the hotel had a lax system in place for security, what with master keys just hanging about for anyone to grab. And then there was the strange odor on the carpet in Marian Fitch's room. But that was it.

I was so thrilled to be back in good form with Detective Briggs, I almost didn't care that the trip to the hotel revealed nothing critical. Although, I did feel for Briggs. He was deep in thought the entire way back to Port Danby. He was in a race against time with this case. Most of the people from the fair would be leaving soon. And everyone was going in a different direction.

On my way back from the police station, I stopped by the Corner Market to buy a precooked hardboiled egg for Kingston. He'd had a rough day. I knew after the scene at the fair, he would be feeling melancholy. And there was nothing worse than a depressed crow.

I headed straight back to the shop with my hard-boiled egg. I had created a chalkboard display for my Thanksgiving centerpieces and decided to place it out on the sidewalk for people to see. I needed to start taking orders or risk not having them finished by the holiday.

Lester was standing in the table area in front of his shop contemplating something as I walked past.

"Hey, Lester, what's got those gears spinning?"

"Hey, Lacey, just trying to figure out something to spruce these tables up for the holidays."

"I've got Thanksgiving centerpieces for sale," I said with a laugh.

Lester's eyes rounded beneath his mop of white hair. "What a great idea!"

"No, I was just kidding, Lester."

His slightly hunched over shoulders drooped under his Hawaiian shirt. "So you don't have any centerpieces for sale?"

"I do but they are for Thanksgiving tables. They are far too big and elaborate for your small coffee tables. There wouldn't be any room for people to place their beverages. And they are far too expensive for a mere sprucing up for the holidays. How about a vase with a single orange rose or one of those pop-up paper turkeys?"

"Paper doesn't hold up on foggy days."

"Hadn't thought of that. Well, think about the rose idea. It's simple and cost effective."

"Possibly too simple," he mumbled as I opened the door to my shop.

I glanced over to Elsie's side to see what she had done to spur on Lester's new quest for table sprucing. She had placed hand-knitted red, orange and yellow placemats around each table. I knew Elsie did some knitting on the side between rising at three in the morning to bake, selling treats and running her five miles a night, but I had no idea how talented she was. The knitted placemats were beautiful and colorful . . . and highly impractical. I couldn't imagine they would last long in the coastal air and beneath messy bakery customers. I glanced back toward the Coffee Hutch. Poor Lester was still standing outside. He was nibbling on the edge of his finger, a habit I'd caught him doing more than once.

I walked into the shop. Kingston swooped down from his perch and danced along the edge of my work island. I had a sensitive nose, but Kingston's sense of smell was preternatural. He had smelled the egg before I'd taken two steps into the shop. And it was inside a plastic container and a paper bag.

I patted his head, but he was in no mood for a caress. His shiny black eyes and beak were focused on the bag in my hand.

"To your perch. I don't want egg smeared all over my work space."

The crow shot back to the perch. He reminded me of an old man with a sharp, crooked nose pacing with his hands behind his back as he trotted back and forth on the wood. I crumbled the egg into his dish and went to the sink to wash my hands.

I was still thinking about Lester and his quest for pretty table adornments. Maybe I could make a smaller, pared down version of my centerpieces for his tables. Of course, then I would probably earn a cold shoulder from Elsie or, even worse, she would stop bringing me luscious samples to taste. Ugh, those two and their table competition.

I decided it was time to put my sample Thanksgiving centerpieces on display in the window. I carried each one out from the cooler I'd had installed in the back closet. I placed each one on an upside down milk crate in the window. I walked outside to look at them.

I had to say I was rather proud of them all. My customers would have one of three displays to choose from, starting with the Berry and Orchid Splendor, a rustic wooden box overflowing with bronze colored mums, ivory orchids, sage green oregonia and dried red berries. My Harvest Basket centerpiece was a less organized, slightly wild collection of tangled huckleberry stems, burgundy striped Nigella pods and cream colored peonies. For a touch of glitz, I'd added in gold painted walnuts and a bright yellow tartan ribbon. The last choice was perfect for the more fastidious host or hostess. I called it Simple Elegance. I'd surrounded a tall glass candle holder with yellow sunflowers, apricot roses, bright green leather leaf fern and sparkling white baby's breath.

"See, that's what I need," Lester said over my shoulder. "But you're right. They would take up too much space. Maybe a pared down version?" he suggested.

"I'll see what I can do, Les."

"Thank you, Lacey. You're a peach." With his dilemma apparently solved, he walked briskly back into his coffee shop. Seemed as if I was being dragged back into the table war whether I liked it or not.

The food fair was still going strong down in the town square. My gaze washed down Harbor Lane. Detective Briggs' car was still parked out front. I was sure he was poring over his notes looking for something to further the investigation. I had been meaning to check out Marian's Sugar Lips Cookbook online just to see if anything of interest popped out at me.

Pleased with my window display, I went back inside and headed into my office. A quick search led to the bookstore page for Marian's book. It had thousands of reviews. Some glowing. Some less than glowing. The cover of the book was white. For some reason, Marian had decided to put her own image front and center, holding up a plate of what appeared to be hazelnut bombs. The severe black color of her hair and the red lips just didn't say cookbook to me but then some people just couldn't get enough of themselves.

I scrolled through some of the reviews. Most people posted only with first names or screen names, but as I rolled the mouse one review caught my attention because it had been written in bold italics. Sure enough, it was from SourGrapes. It was a one star, of course. The person again blasted Fitch for being a phony who couldn't bake her way out of an open door. I clicked on the website link on Fitch's author page. As I searched through the comments, SourGrapes showed up all over the place. Always angry. Always negative. And always in bold italics.

The goat bell rang, signaling I had a customer. I got up from my desk. The investigation would have to wait. I had festive centerpieces to sell.

CHAPTER 23

$\mathcal{I}$ sat at the kitchen table, sifting through my mail as I finished up my spinach salad. Nevermore was curled up on the chair next to me giving his fat paws a good cleaning. I got up and delivered my bowl to the sink. Somehow, I'd managed to get talked into an evening walk with Elsie. She hadn't had enough time for her five mile run and insisted she wouldn't be able to sleep if she didn't at least take a walk. I was sure her walk was brisk and energetic like her run, and still, I'd said yes. I was fairly certain my *yes* answer came from guilt. After I told Lester I'd create some centerpieces for his table, it had been chipping away at me like an annoying pick ax. It wasn't long after that when Elsie came in looking for an evening walk partner. Her husband, Hank, was out of town again on business. I had finally met him a few weeks back for the first time. I had started to think the man didn't exist. But then, *boom*, there he was one day standing in my shop, a tall, broad-shouldered man with distinguished gray sideburns and a kind smile, looking perfectly suited to the fit, energetic woman standing next to him. Elsie insisted that his long trips away had been the best thing for their marriage.

The sun had long since set, and only thin, bluish clouds traipsed along the horizon. It was brisk outside, but a nice night for a walk. I bundled up in a coat, scarf and knitted beanie, a cocoon that I was sure would earn a hearty laugh from Elsie. That woman had no problem running a loop in shorts and a sleeveless tank shirt, even in an icy evening drizzle.

I tied up my walking shoes and grabbed a flashlight from the kitchen drawer. After the power outage, I'd purchased four flashlights and placed them in various convenient locations around the house.

I patted Nevermore on the head to say good bye. He barely lifted his big cat head to acknowledge me.

Elsie lived a few blocks away. Since my street, Loveland Terrace, was at the top of Myrtle Place, it only made sense that I walk down to her house and we journey out from there. I was only halfway down my driveway, bundled up and illuminated with my flashlight, when a whistle drew my attention back to the house. Or the neighbor's house, to be more accurate.

"Where are you off to, my adventurous friend?" Dash called from his porch.

"I'm off for a walk with Elsie."

"No haunted manors, eh?"

"In the dark? Nope. I'll be staying clear of haunted manors. Good night, Dash."

"Be careful and have fun."

I continued down to Elsie's house. She opened the front door before I had a chance to knock. She was holding a picture in her hand. She'd actually pulled on a sweatshirt but was still wearing jogging shorts, leaving her muscular legs bare. "Thought you'd want to see this before we headed out."

I stepped into her house. It was always jarring to step into Elsie's house and not smell sweet, buttery treats. Tonight was especially so. It seemed she'd made something with tomatoes, garlic and onions.

Elsie had taken much more care in decorating the bakery than her home. It was cozy and inviting enough, but it lacked any of the frills and vibrant colors of the bakery.

"Come here to the light. I have a picture of the pastry chef class." Elsie pulled on her reading glasses. I wished I'd brought mine. Each smiling face was sandwiched between a tall white chef's hat and an equally white chef's coat. It was easy to pick out Elsie's spunky grin.

I pointed at her. She had hardly aged. "You look exactly the same, and you are practically swimming in that white coat."

"Yes, they couldn't find one small enough. They were going to order me a children's size, but I decided to forgo the humiliation and just drown in the coat. I rolled the sleeves up to my elbows. Not very practical for working with dough but I managed. This picture was taken the week before I hurt myself and had to quit the class." She pushed it under the light in her living room. "Do you see any familiar faces?"

I ran my eyes across the photo. "Ah ha. Marian Fitch. She's easy to spot. The only one without a smile." I moved to the next face. Her thin red hair streamed out from the tight rim of her hat. "Twyla is standing next to Marian. I suppose this was taken before the Hazelnut Bomb fiasco."

"Oh yes. I kept in touch with a few of the other students, and they said that Twyla was devastated after she lost the lawsuit. When the judge made her pay legal fees for Fitch, Twyla had to declare bankruptcy. She left the chef world completely and worked in a bank or something. She only got back into the food business recently."

"So Twyla had good reason to hate Marian."

"I'd say so, yes. But then a lot of people hated Marian Fitch. Is Detective Briggs any closer to solving the case? I just assumed it was her odd-ball nephew. She treated him abominably. Probably years of pent up anger in that relationship."

"I'm sure there was." I lowered the picture down but Elsie stopped me.

"No, look at it again. There is one more face that you've seen at the fair."

I scanned the faces again. "Is that Celeste Bower?"

"Yes it is. She was kind of a stand-offish type too. She and Marian got along well, but I think they had a falling out." She put the picture down. "We should probably head out on that walk before it gets too late."

I raised up my flashlight. "I'm armed with light and tucked in for warmth."

"I see that." Elsie was holding back an amused smile as she looked me up and down. "You're ready for a walk around the North Pole with all those layers."

We headed to the door.

"I'm a little surprised to see you in a sweatshirt," I noted as we walked outside.

"Since we're just walking, I figured it wouldn't hurt." We headed down Myrtle Place. The crape myrtle trees that lined both sides of the road had nearly shed all their foliage. The same trees would provide the street with a pink and white parade of fluffy popcorn shaped blooms in summer. I looked forward to it.

We passed the Graystone Church Way turnoff. The old church sat in silence with only a few lights shining through the stained glass windows. Sitting on its grassy knoll, it looked like an opening scene for one of those homey historically set movies about pioneers or some small western town. The old cemetery with its tilted headstones of various shapes and sizes only added to the movie set image.

Most of the people buried at the rear of the cemetery, where stone angels and family plot markers jutted up from the grass, had been entombed for many years. The newer graves, like the one for Beverly Kent, were near the front of the grounds with modern, polished stones to mark the graves.

"Elsie, I haven't walked through the graveyard much. Did they bury the Hawksworth family here at Graystone Church?"

"Yes, of course." We stopped just outside of the cemetery. "See that area in the back corner that is fenced off with black wrought iron?"

I squinted through the darkness and saw a glint of the wrought iron in the moonlight. "Where the big angel statue is sitting?"

"Yes, that's it. That is the Hawksworth family plot." An icy wind rolled across the graveyard right then, sending a simultaneous shiver through both of us. We looked at each other with round eyes.

"Do you think that was a spirit?" Elsie asked with a laugh.

"Well, we are standing at the edge of a graveyard. Come on, I think I've seen enough of it too."

CHAPTER 24

I loved being my own boss. I could make decisions about my business on my own with no input or argument or unwanted opinion. I'd gone to sleep deciding that I would open up the shop for a few hours on Sunday. Even though my cut flower supply had been virtually wiped out by Marian's bereaved fans, I hoped that some of the locals would stop in to order a Thanksgiving centerpiece. I'd taken two orders after I'd set the samples out and was thrilled to have people notice them right away. Without any extra help yet in the store, I would have to limit the orders to twenty or twenty-five. Any more than that and I'd run out of time and materials.

After Elsie and I had walked to the lighthouse and back, an exhausting journey with a woman who moved at twice the pace of the average mortal, I'd asked Elsie if I could borrow the pastry class photo. If time permitted, I would walk it down to the police station. It was probably worthless for the investigation, but I thought Briggs might want to see it anyhow, just to give him an idea of who knew Marian even before the food fair. Sometimes those seemingly dormant histories came back to life again. Especially for someone like Marian, who had apparently made a lot of enemies in the past few years.

I planned to only be gone a few hours, so I left Kingston at home with Nevermore. The two got along well, but I always kept Kingston in his massive cage when I wasn't home, just in case Nevermore decided it was time to take out the annoying guy with the black feathers and loud morning caw.

The morning air was extra salty and brisk. Some ominous looking clouds hung low over the water. Otherwise, it seemed like the perfect day for a bike ride. I rolled my bicycle out of the backyard and climbed on. My legs were still tired from having to sprint walk to keep up with Elsie, but the trip to town was mostly downhill.

I rode down Myrtle Place and took a moment to enjoy the cool air on my face as I coasted along. There were a few cars from locals attending Sunday service parked along Graystone Church Way. I stopped to admire the church. It looked far more like a church and less like a movie set in daylight. And the surrounding graveyard didn't seem quite as creepy either. I decided a quick detour to the Hawksworth family plot would not delay my morning too much.

I turned down the small dead end street that led to the church entrance. Graystone Church, with its quaint single steeple, was neither gray nor stone. With the exception of three arched windows on the front and a line of rectangular windows drawn along each side, the entire church was covered with cocoa and earthy brown shingles. Pale yellow storm shutters that could be opened and closed like mini blinds crossed over the stained glass windows on each side of the steeple, and the steeple itself was coated in narrow charcoal slate tiles. The only concession to a walk on the wild side were the two bright red doors leading into the church.

The graveyard, on the other hand, was filled with gray tombstones, which might have been the reason for the ill-fitting name. I left my bicycle on the side of the path and walked through the stones to the fenced-in plot at the rear of the cemetery. The black wrought iron fencing around the Hawksworth family plot had been recently painted with a shiny black lacquer, a color that looked stark compared to the speckled gray stones behind it.

Two white columns supported a pretend Greek style portico

across the top of the massive Hawkworth stone. The family name had been carved in fancy script. Below the surname were the names Bertram and Jill. There were two smaller plots and less impressive headstones on each side of the larger one. I walked along the fence and craned my neck to read the names and dates. Apparently, the horrible tragedy took place in 1906. Phoebe Kate Hawksworth was fifteen years old when she was murdered by her father. Next to her was a headstone with a train carved in it. William Chandler Hawksworth was twelve according to my mental math. I walked to the other side. Cynthia Elizabeth was only ten. I briefly wondered who'd died first and which of the poor children had to watch their siblings die, and at the hand of their father, no less. I had to quickly push the thoughts from my head. They were too awful to contemplate. The plot next to little Cynthia had an unmarked stone. A family pet? Did they bury pets in those days? Perhaps a champion hunting dog? I'd have to research it and see if Bertram had a dog or another pet who he'd considered important enough for burial in the family plot. Of course if he had, why wouldn't he have had the grave marked? It was yet another mystery to add to the list surrounding the Hawksworth family murder.

A cold breeze tugged a strand of my hair free from the band I'd used to tie it up. I pushed the hair back into place and gazed down at the ocean. Occasionally, I could smell weather coming on, like the distinctive smell of rain or even the bitter, burnt smell of lightning. Those clouds were heading this way. It seemed they were going to fizzle out any of the food fair's remaining activity. That meant people would be cleaning up early, making it even more urgent for Detective Briggs to solve the case.

I headed out of the graveyard and pedaled back up the hill to my house. It seemed I was going to need my shabby little car today after all.

CHAPTER 25

*E*lsie called to me as I turned the key to the door. I pulled the key out and walked over to her shop. "What are you doing here?" I asked.

"I should be asking you the same thing. I had a shipment of ingredients come in on Friday. It's been so busy, I haven't had a chance to unpack the boxes and put the stuff away."

"It has been a busy weekend, hasn't it?" I glanced across the street. "I've hardly seen Lola in days. Yolanda certainly has to be thanked for bringing a lot of business to town this weekend." I turned back to Elsie. "I thought I'd open up for half the day and try and get some Thanksgiving centerpiece orders." I squinted up to the sky. It was half blue and half slate gray. "At least until the rainstorm moves in."

"My phone says it won't start raining until this evening. But then that could change at any second." Elsie had been her usual cheery, energetic and talkative self the night before, but it seemed as if something was off this morning.

"Everything all right, Elsie?"

"Yes, just feeling a little blue because Hank called and said he wouldn't be home for Thanksgiving. It's usually just the two of us. We make it into a nice romantic evening. He starts a warm fire and I bake his favorite yeast rolls and the sweet potatoes with the marshmallow topping. Guess I'll be alone."

Even though I'd spent a week designing and creating centerpieces for Thanksgiving tables, I'd been too busy to think about the upcoming holiday. I'd planned on buying a plane ticket home. I needed to do that today. My mouth had been watering for my mom's cranberry and sourdough stuffing.

"What about Lester? Won't he be alone?"

She rolled her eyes. "After he retired, Lester started a tradition of spending Thanksgiving down at the fire station with the guys who have to work on the holiday."

"That's sweet. Good for Lester. Well, if you want to fly home with me, you're welcome to it. I'm sure my mom would love to have you."

She laughed at the notion as I figured she would.

"Don't work too hard, Elsie." I walked back to the shop and pulled out my chalkboard announcing the centerpiece choices.

I spent a half hour organizing ribbons and cards and doing all the things I'd been neglecting during the hectic weekend. I sat down at my work island to start a list of evidence for the case so far. The hand lotion turned out to be a non-starter, considering just about every person to pass through the fair had some form of it on their skin. There was so little to go on that it made me feel extra bad for Briggs. Apparently, death by an allergic reaction didn't leave much in the way of weapons or marks on the body. It all had to do with that creamer. The killer had to have known that Marian suffered from a lethal peanut allergy and that she never drank coffee without her special creamer. That narrowed the field down to about fifty thousand, the number of followers she had on her blog. Of course that field could technically be narrowed down to the people who were in town or nearby by Port Danby at the time of her death. But that left a pretty wide number as well, considering most of the people participating and visiting the fair knew Marian and the Sugar Lips blog. If only there was something more direct to connect her nephew to the fatal dose of peanut butter. But he was either very good at planning a murder or he wasn't the right suspect.

Peanut butter. That term went through my head once more, and I wrote it down to remind myself to let Briggs know that Twyla, the woman who had suffered near personal and financial ruin all due to Marian Fitch, served fried peanut butter balls at her booth.

The bell on the door rang. I had to hide my surprise when Kate Yardley, the owner of the Mod Frock Vintage Boutique, walked inside. It was the first time she had visited my shop. I had only been to hers twice, once to try on some boots that were no longer available and the second time to try on the boots that I'd worn to the food fair dance.

After a quick hello, she headed straight to the window with the centerpiece displays. It seemed I was about to get my first order of the day.

"Just let me know if you want me to pull them out of the window," I said.

Kate was an extremely attractive woman with curves in all the right places and a face that looked good in any light. She had a terrific sense of style and always looked as if she was ready for a magazine shoot. She mostly dressed in the sixties mod style, the fashion pieces from her shop, and she knew just what to do with the crazy colors of the Twiggy decade. Today she was wearing a tight, short dress that had alternating panels of black and white fabric. She had a small black and white matching clutch to go with it. Kate also changed hair color like most people changed socks. She had recently given up white blonde for a toffee apple brown. And darn if it didn't suit her just as well as the blonde.

Kate Yardley was the one shop owner on Harbor Lane who I'd only formed a casual, acquaintance style relationship with. She didn't seem interested in more, which was fine by me. And from what I'd heard, only through loose rumors, Kate and Dash had dated at one time.

Silently, I hoped she wouldn't ask me about the boots because after the first trial run in them, I was reluctant to put them on again.

"I'll take two of the Simple Elegance."

"Terrific." I pulled out my order book. "I'll write up a ticket."

Kate walked up to the island. "How do you like the boots?"

Darn. "The boots? Oh, they're wonderful. They weren't great for dancing, but otherwise, you know for just kicking around in, especially when I want to look extra groovy, they are perfect."

Kate's hair was teased up on top and her bangs dropped down close to her eyes. The entire look stayed perfectly in place with a helmet of hair spray as she tilted her head in question. She really took the mod thing to an unsurpassed level. "I've worn mine dancing a lot. Why weren't they working for you?"

"Just a little tight in the toes. I'm used to wearing sneakers and sandals."

She nodded. "Your feet are probably just too wide for the boots." Kate was also a master at slipping in insults.

"Or the boots were too narrow," I smiled. "Guess it depends which way you look at it."

"Yes, I suppose so."

I decided to leave the boots topic or risk talking myself out of an order for two centerpieces. "Have you been to the fair to try the treats?" I asked.

"I was just there this morning. First chance I got after the rush of customers all weekend."

"Yes, it's been great for business. I sold all my flowers yesterday for —" I paused when I remembered that I'd sold out of flowers because a woman had died.

Kate was glad to finish for me. "Yes, I saw the flowers on the booth." She didn't add any of the usual comments about how sad or what a tragedy but then I hadn't expected it of her.

"Now that was two Simple Elegance centerpieces. Do you like them just the way they are, or would you prefer any substitutions on the flowers?"

"No, they're fine like that. Do you provide the pillar candles?"

"I don't but I can order you some."

"No actually, I have a place I buy candles. I don't want anything that will overwhelm the aroma of the meal I'm preparing."

I totaled up the receipt. "Are you having a big crowd?"

"Just some friends. You might know one of them—Dashwood Vanhouten?" She asked it as if she wasn't well aware we were neighbors. Interesting that he was going to her Thanksgiving dinner but then he hadn't mentioned any trips to see family. In that case, I was glad he had a place to celebrate. (Well sort of glad.)

"Yes, Dash, of course. Sounds like fun."

"It's just close friends from back when we were a couple. You understand. Otherwise I'd be happy to invite you."

My face popped up in the middle of calculating sales tax. "Oh, no, I wasn't—that wasn't a—I'm flying out to see my parents. I never miss one of my mom's Thanksgiving feasts. I just meant, I'm sure it'll be fun." So it was official and the rumors weren't just loose. Dash and Kate had been a couple, a couple with mutual friends. And now he was spending Thanksgiving with Kate and their mutual friends.

Apparently, I was pressing the pen just a little hard on the receipt pad, and it ripped through. "Oops, thin paper on this pad," I chuckled and wrote the total next to the rip. "What day will you pick them up? I recommend Wednesday. That way I can keep the flowers fresher in my cooler."

"Wednesday at ten?" she asked.

"Perfect." I showed her the total.

"Can I pay now?" She placed her shiny clutch on the island and opened the latch.

"I never turn down a payment."

The purse was cute as heck but impractical in size. She tried to get to her wallet, but there was a folded paper in the way. She huffed in frustration and placed the paper on the island. It unfolded and revealed a recipe for a cucumber facial mask with the Sweet Cherry Pie logo on it. I glanced at it for just a second and then something drew my focus back to the paper.

"A cucumber facial mask?" I asked and used it as an excuse to get a closer look at the paper.

Kate opened her wallet and pulled out her debit card. "It sounded interesting. Here you go."

I stared down at the paper. The font for the recipe was printed in bold italics. I was sure it meant nothing, but I decided to make a mental note of it.

I took the card from Kate. "Thank you and thank you for your business."

CHAPTER 26

Several neighbors and Gigi Upton from the Corner Market put in orders for a centerpiece. My idea to come in on a Sunday had paid off. It was close to noon and my stomach was growling for something to fill it. I went to the front window and looked out. The rain I'd predicted with my nose had been stalled out over the sea. It seemed there wouldn't be rain for a few more hours.

Even so, I decided to drive my car around to the town square. That way if the clouds broke, I could just take off from there and head home. I drove down Harbor Lane. I'd seen Detective Briggs drive past the shop an hour earlier, when I was in the middle of helping Gigi decide between the Berry and Orchid Splendor and the Harvest Basket (she settled on one of each). I was of course dying to know where Briggs was heading when he drove past. I was disappointed I wouldn't be able to stop in and tell him a few of the tidbits I'd picked up since I last saw him. Not that they were worth much.

I parked on Pickford Way, across from the marina. A bitterly cold wind caused some of the smaller moored vessels to bounce off the bumpers running along the pier. It seemed that the storm was imminent. I was glad to now have an ample supply of flashlights in case of a power outage.

Most of the bloggers had braved the blustery weather and kept their booths open. They had to pay a sizable fee to rent a booth and sell foods at the fair, so they wanted to get their penny's worth.

Celeste was covering her chicken coop with a tarp as I walked past. I decided to ask her about a copy of the cucumber facial mask recipe. She was having a hard time tying the tarp to the pop-up coop. The hens weren't too thrilled about the flapping canvas. I scooted around to help her. She startled at first, apparently unaware that I had been standing at her booth. We got the tarp secured.

"Thank you," she said. "They hate the rain."

I was just about to agree and mention my crow's aversion to the rain, but I decided not to bring up the sore subject. Her last encounter with my bird had been rather disastrous.

"I was just stopping by to ask about a recipe for a cucumber facial mask. A friend of mine was telling me about it."

"Yes, of course." She turned around to a file box, thumbed through it and pulled out a copy. She handed it over with a grin. Celeste was much more pleasant when I didn't have a crow hovering around me.

I glanced at it and its bold italics font. "That's it. Thank you so much. Do I owe you anything?"

"Nope, it's complimentary. Although, after you try it, if you could leave a comment or review on my blog that would be great."

"I will do that. Thanks again and looking forward to trying it." I folded the paper and pushed it into my coat pocket. I was craving something tasty but light and decided to stop at the DAB booth for a vegan sandwich.

Byron and Daisy looked much more weary and less enthusiastic than they had a few days ago. Byron had switched out his purple beanie for a black fedora, and he had fashioned some of his beard into tiny braids. "What can I get you?"

"I'd like the vegan special on wheat."

"Oh, sorry, we're down to just flatbread."

"That works."

Daisy was huddled in her coat, sitting on a fold-up chair and reading her phone. It seemed she had checked out for the rest of the fair and it was up to Byron to run the booth. He pulled out his cutting board and a baggie filled with fresh veggies.

"Looks like we'll all be closing up early this afternoon," Byron said as he prepared my sandwich. "That cold storm sort of fits the mood around here today."

"Oh? Because of Marian?"

"That and it seems like we're all stuck in one of those big houses on an island where someone gets murdered and all the guests are eyeing each other suspiciously."

"A who-dunnit movie," Daisy piped up without looking away from her phone.

"That's it. Most of us knew Marian. And she had a lot of enemies. People who had been wronged by her in some way, like Twyla with her stolen recipe and Celeste with her book. But I still think it was her nephew. He was her heir, you know? He's going to be rich."

"I've heard that." It seemed to be leaning toward the obvious, the emotionally abused nephew who stood to gain the most from her death. I glanced over to the Sweet Cherry Pie booth. Celeste was starting to pack up. I scooted closer to where Byron was working on my sandwich. "What about the book?"

He looked up confused. "Oh yeah, that." He lowered his voice. "A few years back, Celeste was about to land a killer book deal with a major publisher. At the last second, Marian Fitch's agent swooped in with the Sugar Lips book proposal. Celeste lost the deal and never found another publisher for her book." He handed me the sandwich. "Daisy and I had the same agent as Celeste at the time, so he told us all about it."

"That's a shame. Must have been a big disappointment to her."

"Yeah, just about everyone here has some horror story connected to Fitch. Daisy and I managed to stay clear of her. Other than her griping that our smoothie blender was too loud at the last fair, we didn't have any run-ins with her."

"That's good." I paid him for the sandwich. "And thank you." I lifted the sandwich, but silently I was thanking him for providing a puzzle piece I'd been missing.

I decided to eat my sandwich in the warmth of my car. I was nibbling away enjoying it when a car pulled up in front of me. Surprisingly, Parker Hermann climbed out of the driver's seat. He looked fairly spry as he lifted the collar of his coat up around his ears and hurried across to his aunt's booth slash memorial shrine. The flowers were working hard to keep their petals in the breeze.

I watched him in the side view mirror as he collected up some of the cards and signs that people had placed on the booth. Most of the other bloggers watched him but no one went up to talk to him. Moments later, he returned to his car with the cards. It seemed he had just come to collect the notes before the rain fell and washed away the sentiments. It was commendable.

I wondered how much longer he would be required to stay in town. It seemed if Briggs didn't get any solid leads or evidence soon, he'd have no choice except to let Parker leave.

Parker started the car and took off around the corner to Culpepper Road. I wondered why he hadn't turned around and headed back toward Mayfield.

I started my car. The sleuth in me said 'follow him'.

CHAPTER 27

I didn't know much about stealthily following someone except from what I'd seen in the movies. In the movies, the pursuer was usually in some shiny black SUV or white unmarked van. My cheap little midsized sedan seemed far better for not being noticed. And even though there was no sun to block out, I kept the visor down over the windshield in case Parker looked in his rearview and recognized me. Not that I didn't have a right to be driving along Highway 48 to Chesterton. But I had, after all, been at the scene of his aunt's murder, and I had been the one to discover her cause of death. (No small feat, I reminded myself.)

I knew Parker had been told to stay in town, but Chesterton was so close to Port Danby Parker probably didn't consider it a problem. Chesterton had far more choices for food and stores. Perhaps Parker was just going stir crazy in the hotel waiting for some word on his aunt's murder, and he decided to take a drive.

I had stayed back far enough to avoid being noticed that a truck had pulled onto the highway from one of the smaller rural roads. The slow moving, shambling old truck must have been carrying a hay bale earlier because pieces of straw and grass flew out of the bed at intervals. The bits stuck to my semi moist windshield and the front of my car.

I had to tilt my head far to the left to see around the truck's big side view mirror. Parker's car was as small and plain as my car. On a busier road, I would have already lost sight of him. Thankfully Highway 48 was just a two way highway with very few cars.

I'd relaxed some, loosening my grip on the wheel, thinking I'd catch up to Parker in Chesterton until his car made a sudden left turn down a road that ran along the coast. I'd only traveled it once on a long bike ride and found that the road ended at a cluster of expensive beach houses overlooking the coast.

Thanks to the hay spitting truck, it took me a minute to reach the turnoff. Parker's tail lights disappeared around the bend just as the first significant drops of rain fell.

I wondered if Parker was just lost and would eventually realize he'd hit a dead end and not the town of Chesterton. Then it occurred to me, I was no longer undercover. There were no other cars on the quiet road, and I, too, would eventually hit a dead end. But I'd gone this far, I wasn't about to turn around and scurry off.

Parker's car reached the paved road that led up to the elegant row of beach houses. They had their own little slice of paradise amongst the evergreens and looking out over the pristine ocean below. I could only assume most of them were vacation houses for extremely rich people, people like Parker's aunt. And now people like Parker himself. But it wouldn't make sense for them to stay in a hotel if they'd owned a beautiful beach house just ten miles outside of Port Danby.

It would have been terribly obvious to follow behind him along the quiet street. Especially since I had no place to go at the end of the cul-de-sac. I pulled off onto a circular dirt area that had been cleared, I assumed, for lost drivers to turn around. It might also have been done purposefully to provide a vista for taking pictures because, even under the dreary sky, it afforded a picturesque view of the ocean below. Tall, deep gray rocks jutted out of the turbulent green water. Even from the distance, I could see sea lions resting on the rocks, waiting for the storm surge to pass.

I parked my car at an angle to get a view of the houses above but realized I could only see the top stories and impressive roof lines. And I'd lost sight of my target completely. I hadn't traveled all that way in inclement weather being pelted by wet hay to miss the end of the story. It might have been a bit premature to refer to the weather as inclement, but my nose and my twenty-year-old broken arm bone told me the heart of the storm was moving in fast.

From the landing where I'd parked my car, I noticed a foot path had been cleared. Railroad ties had been stuck in the ground to provide steps up to the street. It led up through a copse of tall evergreens, thickly trunked trees that would provide a nice cover.

I climbed up the crude steps and walked through the trees. A deep voice drew my attention to the end of the trees, where the small spot of wilderness ended in a steep cliff. Some fencing had been put up for safety, but it hardly seemed enough for the severity of the drop off.

I peered through the trees and spotted Parker across the street in front of a palatial looking mansion with white columns and what I considered to be a gaudy amount of marble and stone. Parker was standing on the driveway staring at the garage as if he was waiting for someone to come out.

Then, with a loud hum, one of the three garage doors opened up. A man walked out who looked nothing like I'd expected from a house with marble and columns. He was tall and had a shaved head with several tattoos around his neck. Even in the cold weather, he had on a tank shirt and shorts. And most of all, he looked kind of sinister with deep set eyes, thick brows and a large square chin.

Parker stood by, looking slightly fidgety, almost nervous or excited as the man disappeared into the garage. Seconds later, a loud rumble shook the birds from the surrounding trees. I stepped back quickly to avoid an anxious scrub jay. I lost my footing and slipped through the loose pine needles, landing hard on my knees. One foot had slipped between the wires on the safety fence. My heart skipped a few beats as I stared down at the ocean waves crashing violently against the rocks below. Some of the debris I'd kicked free with my foot tumbled over the edge and out of sight to the sea below.

I pressed my hand against my chest thinking somehow it would slow my racing heart. I pulled my foot back on the safe side of the fence and pushed to my feet. The loud rumble that had caused the trees to shake, the birds to flee and me to fall had been a sports car. The man who had come out to talk to Parker had backed a bright red, flashy car out of the garage. I was no car expert, but it was easy to see that it was an extremely valuable car.

The first of a series of significant rain drops fell through the branches of the trees as I watched the two men look at the car. As the drops fell faster, the bald, sketchy looking man hurried into the driver's seat and pulled the car back into the garage. He took a few minutes to wipe off any drops with a cloth. Apparently, expensive sports cars weren't waterproof.

Parker had lifted the collar of his coat up again as if that might keep him from getting wet. As the bald man came out of the garage, Parker held his hand out. He seemed to be holding an envelope. The man thumbed through the contents and they shook hands. The man went back inside and the garage door rolled down. Parker climbed back into his car, circled around and drove off.

I kept my face down to avoid the onslaught of cold drops and hurried back to my car.

CHAPTER 28

The rain was coming down at a good clip, but I decided to take the long way around past the marina to see if Detective Briggs was in the office. I wasn't sure what I'd just witnessed, but my highly imaginative mind had gone straight to the most dramatic scenario. Had Parker Hermann paid someone to kill his aunt? It would have been easy enough to give a key to a stranger and have them lace the coffee creamer with peanut butter. In the meantime, Parker took a leisurely shopping tour through town to make sure everyone saw him out and about at the time of his aunt's death. He thought it would give him, the person with the best motive, a perfect alibi. But I wasn't so sure that was going to hold. I was certain I'd seen a payment of some kind pass hands. The man in the extraordinarily expensive beach house certainly didn't look like an investment banker or surgeon or high powered lawyer, the type of person you'd expect to own a house in that exclusive neighborhood. But then maybe I was being blinded too much by stereotypes. Just maybe the man was a big success in the stock industry. Maybe he had invented some important medical device. Or maybe he killed people for a living.

I made a left onto Harbor Lane. I was in luck. Detective Briggs was in the office. I pulled into the diner parking lot. Business was slow for Franki during the storm, and I knew she wouldn't mind me parking there for a few minutes.

My naturally curly hair had suffered the torture of the flat iron this morning only to spring right back into curls in the rainstorm. It seemed extra wild and bouncy as I stepped out of the car and hurried across the street to the police station. The gutters were already turning into mini rivers. I had to leap over the rushing water and onto the sidewalk in front of the station.

I stood under the overhang and tried my best to swipe off some of the water beaded on my coat before stepping inside. Hilda peered up over the counter. She had her headset and speaking device on and was just finishing up giving directions to someone on the other end.

She pulled off the headset. "What brings you out on this gloomy afternoon, Lacey?"

"I was hoping I could get in to see Detective Briggs."

"Thought that might be the case." Then she winked. I wasn't sure how to absorb that gesture, but I smiled in return.

Hilda knocked and poked her head inside the office. "Miss Pinkerton is here to see you."

"Send her in," he answered without hesitation. It seemed my talk with him about Dash had helped put any awkwardness behind us. I was relieved.

Briggs was flipping through a file folder. "Celeste Bower," he said as I walked to the chair.

"What about her?"

"She's the blogger who lost out on the cookbook deal when Fitch's agent swept in and grabbed the contract first."

My shoulders shrank just a bit. "There goes one of the pieces of information I was about to tell you. How did you find out?"

"Some deeper research and a few phone calls. I found out the name of Marian's agent. He'd just heard the news when I called him. But he gave me some background on what happened. One big publisher had put out feelers letting the literary agents know that they were in the market for a good cookbook from one of the many popular food bloggers with a big following. Celeste's following was big, but not nearly as big as Marian's with her Sugar Lips site. Which, from what I can deduce, was mostly due to the success of the Hazelnut Bomb donut. Along with some of the publicity that went with it. Guess it's true that any publicity is good publicity. Celeste's book got into the publisher's hands first. They were just about to ink a mid six figure deal with her when Marian's agent dropped her cookbook proposal onto the editor's desk. It seemed the actual recipes didn't matter much. Marian had over a million followers on Facebook, almost three times as many as Celeste."

Briggs dropped the side of the folder and sat back. His longish hair was slightly disheveled. It seemed he had been out in the rain. "How did you find out it was Celeste?"

I sighed contentedly. "I just asked. The two kids at the vegan booth had the same agent. Well, I didn't exactly ask. Byron just happened to mention it. But your way was effective too." I flashed him a satisfied grin.

"Yes, it just took up a lot of my time, and time is not a luxury I have at the moment."

"Losing a lucrative deal like that would be devastating, no doubt. But how long ago did this happen?" I asked.

"Three years ago. And yes, it seems like any anger would have worn off by now. Still, it puts a possible motive on Celeste Bower. Unfortunately, it's not enough to keep her in town. Or anyone else, for that matter. The rain cut the fair short today. Yolanda told me most of the bloggers are leaving town tomorrow morning."

I wiggled my bottom on the chair and sat up straight. "It might not matter if the bloggers are leaving because I saw something today that I think shines a suspicion spotlight back on Parker Hermann."

He squinted an eye to see if I was kidding. "You do?"

"I do. I was sitting at the park eating my flatbread vegan sandwich. Very good, by the way. Anyhow, I was in my car because it was cold and icky outside. And while I was parked on Pickford Way, Parker drove up in his car. He hopped out and collected some of the cards and handwritten sentiments the fans had put on the memorial. Which I thought was genuinely thoughtful."

"Or he wanted to make sure the fans weren't insulted by seeing their cards left in the rain. Remember, the Sugar Lips brand will live on even without Marian Fitch. Parker will benefit from that brand for years, until his aunt's legacy finally fades away for good."

"That's the other less heartwarming explanation for his actions. But it was what he did afterward that didn't make sense. Parker climbed in his car and took off toward Culpepper Road."

"The opposite direction of Mayfield," Briggs noted.

"Exactly. That's what I thought too."

"Wait," he said and squinted at me again, "did you follow him?" His tone let me know that he was not going to be happy with my answer. But if I didn't confess to following him, I'd have nothing of interest to tell him. And I was sure I had a golden nugget of evidence this time.

I ran my finger along the edge of his desk and watched my finger's progress rather than look Briggs directly in the eye. I could almost feel the front edge of the lecture I was about to get, but I forged on.

"There was some following, yes. But I kept at a safe distance," I added quickly.

His chair squeaked as he sat forward and rested his arms on his desk. "Lace—I mean, Miss Pinkerton, if our hunches turn out right and Parker killed his aunt that would make him, at the very least, a person capable of murder. It was dangerous for you to follow him."

I twisted my mouth to the right and left and waited for him to finish. Then I hopped right into the rest of my story. "There really was no danger, Detective Briggs. Unless, of course, you count my foot slipping past the safety barrier on the edge of a steep cliff."

His dark eyes rounded. He was just about to speak, but I put up my hand to stop him.

"That had more to do with startled birds than following Parker so let's just forget it. Obviously I survived because I'm sitting here. As you might have theorized, I had to get out of my car at one point to spy—" I cleared my throat. "To keep my eye on the suspect." That comment earned me one of the detective's wry yet undeniably pleasing half grins.

"And where was the *suspect* at this point?" he asked.

"Parker pulled up to one of those posh beach houses off Highway 48."

"Beacon Cliffs?" he asked.

"I think that's what the sign said. Anyhow, he waited in front of a massive house that was draped in marble and stone. A shady looking man walked out."

"How so?"

I stared at him not sure how to proceed. "There wasn't anything extraordinary. He just walked out one foot in front of the other. Like most bipedal mammals."

He laughed and shook his head. "No, I mean how was he shady? You said he looked shady?"

My cheeks warmed. "Oh, I see. His head was shaved and he had tattoos. He was dressed as if he'd just left the local tavern at closing time. Certainly not who I expected to walk out of the house."

Briggs nodded. "You have a point. What did Parker do with this shady looking guy?"

"Not much. The guy pulled his loud, expensive sports car out of the garage, and seconds later, drove it back inside. The rain had started to fall by then, so I guess he didn't want it to get wet."

"That hardly sounds like something that implicates Parker in his aunt's murder."

I scooted toward the edge of my seat. "I'm getting to that part. Before Parker left the man's driveway, he handed him an envelope. I think there was money inside. A lot of money. It was thick, and the man thumbed through it before going back into his house."

I wasn't overwhelmed by Briggs' reaction. I was hoping that he would at least sit up straighter or write something down in his notebook. He did neither.

"Interesting." That was his total response.

My shoulders deflated. "What if he paid someone to put the peanut butter in the creamer so he could be seen in town and have an alibi?"

"I'm not writing off that possibility, Miss Pinkerton. And I'll certainly ask him about it—without letting on how I know about the transaction," he added.

A knock sounded on the door, and Hilda popped her head inside. "Mr. Hermann is here to see you, Detective Briggs." She lowered her voice. "He looks angry."

CHAPTER 29

*P*arker Hermann did look angry but the way he carried himself made him look comical. There was a stern glower on his small pasty face. "Detective Briggs," he said sharply. "I would like to know what's going on with my aunt's case. It seems you aren't getting anywhere, and I've got things to do. I need to get my aunt back home for burial. I've made arrangements for her remains to fly out on Tuesday, and I will be on that plane."

A person could walk in throwing flaming arrows and hurling death threats and I was sure Detective James Briggs would still stay smooth as polished glass. Sometimes, it seemed I was the only person who could occasionally rattle him or get him to work up some level of emotion.

"Miss Pinkerton," Briggs said calmly, "if there's nothing else, I need to talk to Mr. Hermann." He gave me the slightest brow lift. "I have a few questions for him."

I got up. "Of course and thank you for listening to—to my proposal for the thing we were discussing."

"You're welcome."

I walked out and shut the door after tamping down the urge to leave it ajar. I decided instead to make small talk with Hilda, who looked lonely in the front office. I noticed she was looking at a recipe for pumpkin pie as I walked past her computer. She buzzed me out of the gate, but I lingered at the counter.

"My mom uses real pumpkin for her pie," I said as I straightened up some of the flyers and forms on the counter. "It takes a lot of extra time but so worth it."

"I tried that once," Hilda said. "But I nearly set the oven on fire with pumpkin juice oozing all over the place. I find that the canned stuff is just as good as long as you add in the right spices. And the crust needs to be just right, not too tough or too crumbly. That's my husband's favorite part."

"I do love a good crust. My mom sprinkles cinnamon sugar on hers. It's making my mouth water just thinking about it."

"So you'll be heading home for Thanksgiving?" Hilda asked.

"Yes. Looking forward to it."

"My three kids will be showing up for my feast too. It's the one day I don't mind standing at the stove all day. I think I'll try something new with the pumpkin pie though." She clicked her mouse and the printer came to life. She pulled the recipe off the printer and showed it to me. "It's a pumpkin pie cheesecake combo."

I browsed the ingredient list and nodded. "I've found you can't go wrong when the recipe contains cream cheese."

Hilda laughed. "See, that's what I thought."

The door to Briggs' office opened and Parker swept out, looking only a little less angry. Detective Briggs stepped out to watch Parker leave and then turned to me. "I had a feeling you might still be here."

I motioned to Hilda. "We were talking about pumpkin pie recipes. Are you heading out of town for Thanksgiving?"

"Haven't decided yet." He pushed the buzzer for the gate. "If I could see you for just a second, I have some information."

A tremble of enthusiasm raced through me as I walked through the gate. "Did my adventure pay off?" I asked as I followed him into his office.

He didn't walk all the way around his desk but instead just leaned against the front of it. He rested his hands back on the edge, highlighting the impressive width of his shoulders. "I told him an officer saw him heading out on Highway 48 today and asked him what business he had out that direction."

"And his answer?"

"Well, after the red rage cleared from his face, he asked if he was being followed or if he was under investigation? And he asked if he should hire a lawyer. I told him it was just a simple question. He had a pretty simple, straightforward answer. He said he was out that way looking at a sports car he's going to buy. He left the man with a sizeable down payment until his aunt's living trust is freed up. It seems he's out spending his inheritance."

"Do you believe him?" I asked.

"Let's just say that I've been at this for awhile, Miss Pinkerton. During that time, I've become pretty good at telling a lie from the truth. He answered without hesitation, and he looked me right in the eye. There was no fidgeting, no extra blinking or change to his voice. I think he was out at Beacon Cliffs looking at a car."

I pulled in a deep, disappointed breath. "Thought I was on to something."

"Yes, I know you did. And don't do anything dangerous like that again."

"Why, if I didn't know any better, I'd say you were worried about me, Detective Briggs."

"I worry about all the citizens of Port Danby, Miss Pinkerton. Keeping everyone safe is part of my job."

"All right then. I won't take your concern personally." I headed out.

"Oh, Miss Pinkerton, I'll be heading to the hotel at six in the morning to talk to the employee who took the coffee order. That's when his shift starts. I think he's going to be a key witness. If you're interested—"

"Yes," I said probably too quickly. "I'd like to go, if you don't mind."

"I thought you might. By the way, just because he was out buying a car today doesn't mean Hermann is off the suspect list. In fact now that I see how anxious he is to spend his new fortune, I'll be looking even closer at him."

"So my adventure did help a bit?"

"A bit. Good night, Miss Pinkerton."

"Good night, Detective Briggs."

CHAPTER 30

he cold rain outside made Nevermore decide that just curling up next to me on the couch wasn't enough. Instead, the cat burrowed beneath the plush throw I'd thrown over my legs. Even with socks on, my feet were cold. Winter was in the air, it seemed. Elsie had told me that Port Danby got a nice little 'hug of snow' in December and January. Even with my chilly toes wiggling beneath a blanket, I was looking forward to it. Occasionally, there would be snow fall in the city, but it took only hours before the sparkling white flakes turned to gray mush on the streets and side-walks. Just like with rain, snow in the city was nothing but a major inconvenience. It would be fun to have snow that I could actually enjoy like I had as a kid, when I'd spent hours in the front yard trying to construct a snowman. The best part of that adventure was going back inside, limbs and precious nose frozen, to sit down to my mom's homemade tomato soup and grilled cheese sandwiches. That little spark of nostalgia prompted me to pick up the phone and call my mom. I needed to pin point the dates for my plane tickets.

I picked up the phone and dialed her.

"Hello, my precious girl, I was just about to call you."

"Then we must have been on the same wavelength. I need to figure out what day to fly out there for Thanksgiving."

Silence. My mom was never silent during a phone call. With the delay on a cell phone, she tended to talk right over me. But this was silence. I pulled the phone away from my ear to look at it. I was still connected.

"Mom?"

"Yes, dear, I'm here. I thought you would be staying in Port Danby for the holiday."

"And miss your Thanksgiving feast? Why would I do that? Or maybe you and Dad have other plans?"

"Lacey, that's just it. Remember that nice couple Dad and I met on the cruise, Joan and Harvey? Well their kids are all out of town too, and they won't be coming in for Thanksgiving. They have a beautiful mountain cabin overlooking a lake. They've invited Dad and me up for the long weekend."

"That's very nice," I tried to sound enthusiastic, but my mind was absorbing the notion of no pumpkin pie or sourdough stuffing.

"No," she said suddenly. "We'll just tell them we can't make it. You fly home, dear, and we'll cook up a big feast."

"Don't be silly, Mom. You can't miss out on a wonderful weekend like that. I'm glad you and Dad found some friends. You have to go. I'll be fine here. I've got lots of friends. I might even cook a feast myself. I think I know most of your recipes by heart. Even though nothing will taste the same if you don't make it."

"Are you sure, Lacey? I don't want to leave you alone on Thanksgiving."

"I won't be alone. You and Dad go and have a good time. Just remember to pack warm clothes. And don't forget to pack Dad's Thanksgiving pants. The ones with the elastic waistband."

Mom laughed. "There is no way he is wearing those ridiculous clown pants on this trip. He'll just have to maintain some self control at the dinner table. If you're sure then, sweetie."

"Yes. Absolutely. I'll make plans here. Besides, Christmas is just around the corner. I'll fly home for that."

"I'll be looking forward to it," she said.

"Have fun and I want to hear all about it when you get back."

"We will, dear. And let me know if you need me to email you some recipes. I have them mostly in my head, but I can just type them out for you."

"I'll take you up on that, Mom. Good night."

"Nightie night."

I hung up. It had been a long while since I'd felt the heaviness of homesickness, but I could still recognize it. I was happy for my parents though. They were getting out and making friends. It was wonderful. I would have been even happier if it didn't mean missing my mom's feast and her corny little resin turkey place settings. And Dad sitting on the couch yelling at the football players on television while snacking on cut vegetables and dip. But I was a grown up now. Maybe it was time to start some of my own traditions in my new town.

I picked up the phone again and dialed Elsie.

"Hey, Pink, I was just trying a new cinnamon streusel cupcake recipe. It's delicious."

"Do you ever rest?" I laughed. "The reason I called is that it just so happens that I'm going to be all alone on Thanksgiving. My parents have some new friends. Apparently I'm just a big drag on their social life. You mentioned that Hank wouldn't be in town. Would you like to come here for dinner?"

"Yes! Fun! I can make my special brioche rolls, and I make a pecan pie that melts in your mouth."

"Mouth watering already. I'll ask Lola too. She didn't seem to have much going on. Her parents are somewhere in Austria or one of those castle filled places."

"Ooh, now I'm excited."

"Me too."

CHAPTER 31

*B*riggs and I had stopped in for one of Lester's morning brews, a rich medium roast with a touch of hazelnut, before heading out to Mayfield. The storm had passed through by midnight, but it had left behind a heavy, bone chilling mist.

I was as excited as a kid heading to an amusement park. It might have just been because my curiosity was in overdrive over Marian Fitch's murder. Or it might have been my elation at having Detective Briggs think highly enough of my sleuthing skills to ask me along. Or it might just have been my peculiar, offbeat definition of fun. It was probably all three.

We pulled into the hotel parking lot. It was still early, a few hours before checkout, when most of the bloggers would be headed off in different directions. At least the main suspect, Marian's nephew, would still be in town for a day.

"The hotel manager left me a message last night to stop at the front desk and talk to—" Briggs reached into his coat and pulled out his notepad. "Brenda, the desk clerk. He said she recently remembered that a woman had come in to ask what room Marian was in on the day of her death. She couldn't tell her, of course. But it might be something."

"That is if Brenda is good at recalling details. She must see a hundred new faces a week at her job."

He glanced over at me. "Someone isn't her usual positive, forward-looking self today."

"Is it that obvious? It seems I've been left out in the cold for Thanksgiving by none other than my own parents. Turns out they'd prefer to spend it with their new friends up in some enchanting mountain lake cabin."

"Those monsters," he quipped.

I elbowed him. "But that's all right. I called Elsie and we're making a dinner at my house. You can come of you like. The food will be tasty because, well . . . Elsie the wonder cook will be in the kitchen. And I've been known to make a tasty green bean casserole or two."

Briggs didn't answer.

"I'm sure you have your own plans. I was just being neighborly."

"Actually, that sounds nice. If you're sure you have enough."

"Yes, of course we'll have enough. See, now I'm back to my starry eyed, Pollyanna self."

"Glad to hear it. I think I need your Pollyanna self on this one because I keep coming up short on leads."

We headed straight to the front desk.

A tall woman with a tightly wound bun and a bright blue turtle-neck sweater beneath her hotel coat was standing behind the counter. Her nametag said Brenda. "May I help you?" she asked.

Detective Briggs discretely showed her his badge. "I'm Detective Briggs and this is my assistant, Miss Pinkerton." I had to work hard not to do an impromptu dance at his referring to me as his assistant. "I'm assuming you are the Brenda I'm supposed to see about a visitor on the day Ms. Fitch died?"

"Yes, that's me." She looked around for another employee. "Mitchell, can you cover the desk for me? I'll be right back." She walked around the counter. "Mr. Trumble said we could use his office for this."

We walked across the cavernous lobby to a small hallway. She knocked on the door with the hotel manager nameplate. After no answer, she used her key and we went inside.

"I'm not sure why this didn't occur to me that day. I suppose it was just because we don't generally have police and coroners show up to the hotel. And poor Mr. Trumble was in such an agitated state that I had to step in and perform some of his duties. So I forgot all about the visitor."

"That's fine." Briggs pulled out his notebook. "Mr. Trumble mentioned that someone who did not have a room at the hotel came in looking for Ms. Fitch's room?"

"Yes. Of course I told her I couldn't give out that information unless the hotel client had left directions to do so. And there were no such orders. She pleaded a bit and then walked away from the counter."

"Can you describe the woman? Was she alone?"

"She was alone. And I don't remember much from the hectic day, but she had red hair and some butterfly tattoos on her forearm."

"Twyla Walton," I piped up.

Detective Briggs wrote down the information. "I remember talking to her the day after the murder." He flipped back in his notes. "She's the one who lost the lawsuit against Fitch for her stolen Hazelnut Bomb recipe." He turned to Brenda. "Anything else? Do you remember if she was carrying anything? How was she acting? Did she seem agitated or upset?"

Brenda rubbed her chin in thought. "I think she was carrying one of those cute little backpack purses. But she didn't seem agitated or upset, at least not until I turned down her request to give out room information."

I played a game in my head and formulated the questions I would ask if I was a detective, and I found I was doing a fairly impressive job of thinking like an investigator. I wondered if Brenda saw Twyla leave the hotel lobby at that point.

Briggs scribbled down a few notes on Twyla's notebook page. "Did you see the woman walk out the exit?"

I was good at this.

"To be perfectly honest," Brenda started, "another customer stepped up to the counter afterward, and I lost track of the woman. I assumed she walked out the exit, but I can't say so for sure."

"Was that the last time you saw her?" Briggs asked.

I didn't think of that one. I suppose that was why he had the badge, and I was just the assistant.

"Things got fairly crazy around here just an hour or so later, when all of you showed up, so I have no idea. I can't remember specifically seeing her, but it was entirely possible."

"Thank you, Brenda. You've been very helpful. If you think of anything else we'll be down in the kitchen area."

"Great. I'll see if anyone else saw a red head with butterfly tattoos that afternoon and let you know." Brenda opened the office door and we walked out.

"Thank you again." Briggs and I headed to the elevator and stepped inside when it stopped at the lobby.

I stepped to the back and blushed lightly as I thought about the moment in the dark in the elevator. It had been such a natural instinct to turn to Briggs when I was scared. I tried not to read anything into my reaction, but it was hard not to.

"I think I forgot to mention that Twyla was serving deep friend peanut butter balls at the food fair."

"Yes, I have that written down on my notepad already. She does have a motive."

"The dance." The words popped out as I turned to Briggs. "I'd forgotten all about Twyla's scene at the dance. She had been sampling far too much craft beer, and she was wavering on the dance floor. Once she left the floor, she headed over to Marian's booth and started yelling at her, telling her she would never forgive her for stealing her recipe and that Marian's cookbook was a fake. It was quite the scene. Marian hardly flinched though. It seemed to just sail right over her. Dash stepped into lead Twyla away." I'd forgotten and used the 'D' word in front of Briggs, but he was too consumed with the case to notice or remark on it.

He pulled out his notepad. "A few of the other bloggers mentioned it along with Parker Hermann. He seemed convinced that Twyla killed his aunt. But a beer fueled rant is hardly enough to make an arrest. Let's see what Vincent, the room service attendee, says."

It turned out Vincent was waiting for us inside the small booth where the complimentary coffee service ran from. Vincent was a fresh faced, just out of his teens looking guy who was desperately trying to sprout facial hair but having a time of it.

Briggs wrote down his full name on his pad. "I know you left town before most of the chaos started and you've been offline all weekend, but do you remember the complimentary coffee orders you took on Friday?"

"They are sort of a blur now, but the order from 801 was definitely a woman. I can remember it mostly because she was talking sort of low and growly, like she was disguising her voice."

"Anything else unusual about the conversation?"

Vincent grinned. "Was I talking to the killer? That is so creepy and so cool all at the same time."

"We don't know if you were talking to the killer." Briggs never lost patience, which was amazing because I was ready to give the kid a pop on the head to concentrate. "Did the person order one coffee? Were there any specifics added to the order, like creamer or sugar?"

"No, she just asked for one cup of the house's special brew, black, to be delivered to Room 801 at five o'clock. Then Neil took it to the room and left it, even though I guess the lady never ordered it." Suddenly Vincent looked a little paler, and he fidgeted with the buttons on his white coat. "I poured the coffee, but there wasn't anything wrong with it. I heard the lady was poisoned or something, but we poured a lot of cups from that—"

Briggs placed a hand on Vincent's shoulder to calm him. "You are not being interrogated. You're not a suspect. You're a witness."

Vincent's shoulders relaxed. "That coffee was the same as always."

"Yes, of course." Briggs sounded disappointed. I wasn't sure what he was hoping to learn from Vincent. Something apparently that would give him some clues into who made the call.

"The call definitely came from Room 801?" Briggs asked.

Vincent pointed out the panel on the wall with each room number next to it. Several of the red lights were flashing next to room numbers, which seemed to indicate they were waiting for service. "Unless something is wrong with that board, it came from Room 801."

"Thank you then, Vincent. You've been very helpful."

"You know there was one thing that I just remembered," Vincent said. "But it probably doesn't matter."

"Any information you have," Briggs said.

"A cell phone rang as the woman ordered the coffee. The ringtone was music of some kind. One of those old time rock and roll guys, but I can't think who right now."

Briggs wrote that detail down with more enthusiasm, his pen scratching the paper as he dragged it across the pad. "Think about it and call me if you come up with the song or the band."

He handed Vincent his card. "Thank you again."

Briggs and I walked back to the elevator. "Old time rock and roll guys," I repeated. "Buddy Holly? Elvis?"

"I'd say we could stand here all day and list them and still never know for sure. Maybe Vincent will come up with it. But now, it's time to go talk to Twyla."

CHAPTER 32

*T*he rain had dampened everything. Most of the bloggers had packed equipment and supplies up the night before. Today was just left for banners and decorations. Yolanda had cleverly given a thirty percent discount on the booth if the person stayed Monday morning to help clean up their section of the fair. It seemed more than half of the people had gone for the discount.

Yolanda was in the town square in her rain boots, jeans and scarf helping pick up trash. Fortunately for Detective Briggs, the two bloggers of most interest had opted for the cheaper booth fee.

Twyla was stacking leftover paper food wrappers in a box as we approached. I let Briggs know that I'd stand somewhere else while he interviewed her. I also assured him, I'd stay within hearing distance. I'd come along with him this far on the case, I wasn't going to miss out when he finally nailed his suspect.

"Ms. Walton, it looks like you're just about ready to head out," I heard him say as I busied myself untying deflated balloons from a nearby tree.

"Yes, just about done here. Have they found out what happened to Marian yet?" she asked.

"Not yet, but we're working on it. And since you brought it up, I wonder if I can ask you a few questions."

Twyla's significant pause made me look their direction. It turned out she was just putting packing tape on a box. She combed back her red hair with her fingers as she straightened with the packing tape on her wrist like a clunky bracelet. "Sure thing."

"I was interviewing a few people at the hotel. It came to my attention that on the day of the murder, a woman with red hair and butterfly tattoos on her arm walked up to the front desk and asked which room Marian was staying in."

I could feel my ear twitching like a horse ear, trying to turn in the direction of the conversation so I could catch every word of her response. But her answer was much simpler and more straight forward than I'd anticipated.

"Yes, I went to the hotel to look for Marian," she said as if she was just shooting the breeze with a friend.

"Why were you looking for her room?" Briggs asked.

"I went there to apologize." I heard some shuffling of canvas and glanced back to see Twyla rolling up her banner. She stopped with the banner rolling when Briggs placed his hand on it to let her know he needed her full focus.

She sighed audibly. "The night of the dance, I had a little too much to drink. I went off like a madwoman telling Marian that she should be ashamed and that she stole my recipe. The next day, after my head had cleared, I regretted my behavior. I couldn't look at her all day during the fair I was so embarrassed. I decided to give the old biddy an apology. I'm sure it's something she has never done in her life, so I figured even though she stole my recipe at least I could show her I was the better human. And the better baker but that's beside the point."

"I see. Did you make it up to her room? Did you get a chance to apologize?" Briggs asked.

I was out of balloons.

"Lacey, yoo hoo, Lacey," Yolanda called across the way. "I could use some help getting balloons down on this side."

I waved. "There's still a lot of things to do over here." Her loud call drew everyone's attention for a moment, which worked in my favor. That way I didn't miss Twyla's answer. I looked quickly around for some other task and discovered that there was trash behind the tree. I skirted around the trunk, contorting my head and neck to listen in.

"No, the woman at the desk refused to give me the room number. I left the hotel and decided to apologize before the fair opened on Saturday. That never happened, obviously."

"Did you know about Marian Fitch's peanut allergy?" Briggs asked the question that I'd had on my lips. It was as if our minds were connected.

"Everyone who knew her, knew about it. It was severe enough that she had to take precautions to not be too close to peanut products. I'll be honest, sometimes I think my subconscious told me to start cooking with peanut butter just because I hated Marian so much. But I would never kill her." She laughed dryly. "I walk around trails of ants because I don't want to hurt them."

"Thank you. I won't take up any more of your time. Except one more thing. Have you ever tasted any of Marian Fitch's special creamer? She talked about it quite often on her blog."

"Creamer? What creamer? I never read her blog."

"Thanks again. I'll let you get back to cleaning up."

I tossed the trash I was holding and hurried to catch up to Detective Briggs. "Well, does your honesty radar think she was telling the truth?" I asked.

"I would say yes. It seems I'm heading back to square one. And after the early start, I think I need another cup of Lester's coffee to get my head thinking straight again. Do you need a lift back home to get your car or bike or bird before you open the shop?"

"That would be lovely. I'm just going to change and put Kingston in the car. Then I'll stop by and grab a coffee with you at the Coffee Hutch. My head needs a little clearing too. Maybe with both of us pumped on caffeine some of this will fall into logical sense, and we can figure out just what happened to Marian Fitch."

CHAPTER 33

*J*t seemed I was going to be a little late opening my shop. The first thing I was going to do this week was get serious about finding someone to help in the store. It was nice being the owner and executive decision maker, but it wasn't so great being the only employee. Hiring help had always been part of my business plan, but I was going to wait until things got moving. Fortunately, things got moving fast. I needed to move up that part of my plan and make it a priority. It would be nice to know I had someone to cover if I was in bed with a flu or busy at a florist workshop. Or helping on a murder case.

Kingston had been antsy on the car ride. He normally stood on the top of the back seat watching out the side windows, but this morning he'd posted himself right up front on the edge of the passenger seat. I'd had little time for him the day before, and the weather had kept him at home on his perch.

I pulled up to the shop. The second I opened the passenger door, he flew out and soared over the trees to stretch his wings.

Detective Briggs was sitting at one of Lester's tables drinking a coffee. I quickly glanced in the direction of the bakery and saw that Elsie had two tables full of customers. Lester did too. The past weekend had been so busy, neither of them had been outside rearranging tables or adding luxury items like plush pillows to their outdoor patios. Lester hadn't brought up the centerpieces either. Maybe things had cooled off in the table competition. Fingers crossed that they had.

Before I'd even reached the table where Briggs sat, Lester poked his head out the door to get my attention.

"Any chance you'll have those fall centerpieces for my tables in the next few days, Lacey?"

Fingers officially uncrossed. "I'll get to work on those today, Les."

He waved and disappeared back into his shop. I had hoped that he'd forget the centerpieces for one big reason. Elsie wasn't going to be happy about them. But now that I'd seen his enthusiastic smile, I needed to make some nice centerpieces for Lester. I'd let Elsie know ahead of time, just to avoid a calamity.

Detective Briggs hopped up and pulled out my chair. I thanked him. He was truly a gentleman. It made me wonder what woman was silly enough to give him up. Or maybe it had been the other way around. No one seemed to know the details of his brief marriage. Not even Lola or Elsie, who between them knew just about everything there was to know about the locals.

Briggs pushed a cup of coffee toward me. "Lester said you like the mocha lattes. I hope you don't mind that I took the liberty to order you one. Or if you'd like something else I could get that."

"This is fine. Thank you." I took a sip of the coffee. It hit the spot. It had been a long morning, and the day had just begun.

I noticed Briggs had his notebook out on the table. He caught me glancing at it and placed his hand on it.

"I was going over all the physical evidence Pritchett and her team found at the scene. There is so little to go on. The one tangible piece of evidence was that lavender hand lotion you detected, but that made just about everyone at the fair a suspect. Otherwise, it was a clean crime. Marian was at her manicure appointment when the call for coffee was made from the room. A female called from the suite, and that female is our perpetrator."

He flipped open his notebook and stopped. "I don't want to take up any more of your time, Miss Pinkerton. I appreciate all your help with this, but I know you have a business to run."

"It's fine. I opened yesterday for a few hours. After the busy weekend, today will be slow. Especially for flowers. Go on." I motioned toward his notes.

"The woman had to know about the peanut allergy and Marian's special creamer."

"And that could have been anyone who read her blog." I sat up straighter. "Which reminds me. Bold italics."

Briggs squinted an eye as he looked at me over his coffee cup. "Did you just say bold italics?"

"Yes. I forgot to tell you this. That whole thing with Parker meeting that man and handing him an envelope of money pushed this detail out of my head, but it might be important. When I was perusing Marian's blog looking for clues, I noted that one frequent commenter was particularly nasty and negative toward Marian. Of course, every blog and site has its trolls, but this person seemed to loathe Fitch and her entire Sugar Lips brand."

"Sour grapes?" he asked.

I pointed at him. "You noticed her too."

He nodded. "She even took the time to leave a negative review on Marian's cookbook."

I sat back with a proud grin. "I'm thinking just like a detective. So you noticed the font too?"

"Font? What font?"

"Bold italics. It's unusual to see both. Yes, some people use bold because they want to make a point or possibly because they have an inferiority complex. I mean whoever really knows the true psychological source behind the bold type user. And some people use italics because it adds a bit of flare to the words. So if you write something rather dull and pedestrian, the italic font makes it look more poetic. But bold italics you just don't see that often."

There was that amused half smile of his that I found very charming. "And what is your theory for the lack of people using bold italics? The rare combination of inferiority with the desire to be poetic?"

I laughed. "Nope. Just that it takes two steps to make bold italics. You have to click the B and the I."

He shook his head as the half grin developed into a full smile. "Just when I think I have the inner workings of your mind figured out, you throw me totally off track."

"Is that good or bad?"

"It's good. It keeps me on my toes. Something I need in this job." His phone rang, interrupting the light, mildly flirtatious moment.

He pulled it out. "Detective Briggs here." He sat forward to block out some of the noise from the seat. "Yes, Vincent, go ahead." He pulled out his pen with his free hand and scribbled something on the notepad. A somewhat amused expression followed. "Is that it? Thanks, Vincent. That helps. If there's anything else, just give me a call." He hung up. "Turns out when you're nineteen, Tom Petty is an old time rock and roll guy."

I laughed. "Let's not tell Tom that." And then it clicked. "Wait. Tom Petty? *The* Tom Petty?"

"Not sure if there's any other but yes, Tom Petty." He looked at his notepad. "The ringtone was from his song Free Fallin'. Please tell me that helps us solve this case because everyone is getting on airplanes and climbing into rental cars and the murderer is going along with them."

"Celeste Bower, the woman who lost out on the cookbook deal, was wearing a Tom Petty concert t-shirt the day she was setting up her booth. I accidentally overheard Dash and her talking about the concert. She was telling him that she and her sister were obsessed with his music."

"Figures Dash was there making small talk with all the women bloggers," he said unnecessarily to which I responded with the appropriate annoyed expression.

"We should probably hurry," I said.

"We?"

"I just gave you a major piece of the puzzle."

"Right. Let's go to the town square and see if we can find her. If not, Yolanda has a list of where people were staying. She gave me a copy, but it's in my office." He looked at his watch. Checkout is at eleven and it's ten now, so we might just catch Celeste before she leaves."

We rounded the corner onto Pickford Way and saw Yolanda helping to roll up a banner for the Sandwich Queen booth. Briggs and I hurried across to her.

"Mrs. Petri, may I see your list that shows where the fair participants are staying?"

Yolanda looked confused as she pulled the list out of her pocket. It had names, motels and contact numbers listed next to each participant's name. Good old overly organized Yolanda.

As Briggs scanned the list, I spotted Celeste just leaving the town square with a few boxes. I tapped his arm and motioned that direction.

My thought was to walk right up to her and ask about her ringtone, but Briggs did something that reminded me why I was still the amateur and he was the professional. He pulled out his phone and found the contact number for Celeste. Seconds later, a phone rang.

Celeste stopped, trying to figure out how to answer it with boxes in her hands. An air of letdown fell over us. There was no music ringtone just the standard cell phone ring. Celeste decided to ignore the call and continued on to the motel across the street.

Briggs handed the list back to Yolanda. "Thank you." I hated to hear the disappointment in his voice, but it looked as if we'd hit another dead end.

CHAPTER 34

I hadn't noticed that Kingston followed us to the town square until he swooped over head and landed in the branch of a tree. He seemed to be waiting for me to *not* be watching him, like a kid waiting for the path the cookie jar to be clear of Mom's view.

"Your bird seems to want your attention," Briggs noted.

"Actually, the opposite. He's up to something. I just haven't figured out what." We walked back toward his car. "Have you talked to Parker Hermann today? Is he still planning to fly out with his aunt's remains tomorrow?"

"I'm going to head over to the hotel right now to see if that can be delayed. Although, I'm sure it takes a good deal of planning to have a body transported to another state. I'm not looking forward to telling him that I haven't zeroed in on a suspect yet. And I'm equally not happy to have to let him know he's still on the list and that he may be called back for questioning at any time."

"Oh, Lacey," I heard Yolanda's upset tone from behind. "Your bird just knocked over a trash can."

"Guess my crow just made a beeline for the unguarded cookie jar."

Briggs' brow line crinkled. "What?"

"Just a metaphor I use to describe my bird being naughty." Kingston's wings flapped in excitement as he pulled some trash free and nibbled at some treat he'd managed to find. "I don't want to keep you, Detective Briggs. I'll walk back to the shop."

"I'll let you know what else I find," he said.

I hurried over to the mess on the grass.

The booth was still standing, but it was free of banners and decorations. But from its placement in the square, I knew it had been Celeste's booth. "Not that stale flax seed again, Kingston. You're going to make yourself sick."

I shooed Kingston away and turned back to the mess on the grass. I leaned down to pick up some of the debris. I caught a whiff of something foul. And yet, it was oddly familiar. I picked up some of the discarded seeds and held them to my nose. I winced at the odor. "Dead fish dipped in old paint," I mumbled to myself.

I stood and waved at Kingston. "Go to the shop now."

Kingston looked longingly at the spilled seed for a second and then flew off. I ran toward Briggs' car. He was just about to pull away from the curb.

"Stop, Briggs, I have something. Stop!"

The brake lights went on and the motor turned off. He climbed out of the car, looking more than a little baffled.

I waved him toward the fallen trash. "Over here. This is it. I think I just found the smoking gun."

Briggs followed me to the spot where the seeds had been dispersed in the grass. "Remember that weird smell I noticed on the carpet of the hotel room?"

"I think you called it dead fish paint or something like that."

"Dead fish dipped in old paint. It's a very distinct, unpleasant odor that I had never smelled before. Until now." I reached down and picked up a few seeds for him to smell. He crinkled his nose.

"It smells funny, like oil gone bad."

"To you it's not that strong, but to me, it's enough to make my eyes water. This is what I smelled in the carpet in the hotel room. I'm sure of it. This was Celeste Bower's booth. The flax seeds were for her chickens. On the first day of the fair, I saw her throw the flax away because it was bad. Kingston tried more than once to get at the discarded seed."

Briggs' brown eyes lit up. "If it was in the grass all this time, then she had the smell on her shoes. She tracked the smell into the hotel room."

"Do you think we could go back and take a sample of the carpet. Maybe just a few fibers to double check?"

"I'll make sure of it." He pulled out his phone. "First, I need Officer Chinmoor to put caution tape around this area and have him collect evidence."

Yolanda looked weary and the pile of spilled trash wasn't making her happy. She marched toward us. I walked away from Briggs as he talked to Officer Chinmoor. I stopped Yolanda.

"Yolanda, I'm sorry about the trash spill, but Detective Briggs needs it to stay right there. He's calling Officer Chinmoor right now to tape it off and collect evidence."

"Evidence?" she huffed in disbelief.

"Yes, it's too early to say anything, but you'll have to just ignore this part of the square. Let me say though, Yolanda, you did a spectacular job with this fair. Truly. No one could have done a better job." My flattery was actually the truth. She had done a stellar job, and my words put a big smile on her face.

"Thank you, Lacey. That's nice to hear. I'll let Detective Briggs get back to his police business then."

Briggs hung up as I returned to where he was standing. The black and white patrol car pulled up. It helped that the police station was only two blocks away.

"Good news and bad news," Briggs said. "Mr. Trumble said no one stayed in the suite after all, so we can get in there and cut a few fibers from the rug."

"The bad news?"

"I called the motel to tell them to let Celeste Bower know that I needed to speak to her. They said she'd already checked out. They gave me the color, make and plate for her van. I'm going to give highway patrol a call on our way to the Mayfield Hotel." I followed along with him.

"Unless you need to go, Miss Pinkerton."

"Are you kidding? We're getting close now. I'm sticking to you like a barnacle on a ship's hull until this is solved."

CHAPTER 35

$\mathcal{W}$e were running against the clock. There was still no word from highway patrol that Celeste had been found. But Detective Briggs wasn't too worried. She'd be easy enough to track down if there was evidence to do so. And my gut, or at least my infallible nose, was saying there would be.

Mr. Trumble met us as we walked into the lobby. He had a key to take us up to the room. We stepped into the elevator with him. He was a man who just never seemed comfortable in his own skin, as if any minor thing could set him off. I wondered how on earth he ran a large hotel with hundreds of employees.

"You're not going to damage the carpet, are you?" he asked. "Those suites were only recently remodeled. The hotel owners spared no expense on the carpet and furnishings."

Briggs pulled out the tiny pair of sterilized scissors that were packed in sterile packaging. "Just a few strands with the substance is all we need. You won't miss those fibers, I promise."

Something had occurred to me on the way up. "Mr. Trumble, housekeeping didn't clean the carpets this weekend did they?"

"With a carpet cleaner? No, that's only for stains. But the room was vacuumed and sanitized from top to bottom." His face smoothed with concern as he looked at Briggs. "You told me we could clean for the next guests."

"Yes, I did. And that's fine." The elevator stopped on the eighth floor. We stepped out. We followed the manager to the room. The maintenance cart happened to be sitting outside a room with an open package of light bulbs on top. It seemed light fixtures were being replaced. Sure enough, the master key was right on top of the cart.

"Uh, Mr. Trumble," Briggs said stopping the manager's hurried pace. He pointed at the key on the cart. The maintenance man was inside the room and out of view of his cart and the key. "Just thought I should mention that this is the second time I've noticed that the main-tenance crew leaves the master key out in plain view."

Mr. Trumble looked down at the key and grew visibly paler. He plucked the key from the cart and shoved it into his pocket. Then he led us to Room 801 and opened it for us. "I'll let you do your work. I need to speak to my maintenance man."

We walked inside. I gave Briggs an admonishing look. "Tattle-tale."

"Hey, if it keeps hotel guests from being poisoned by peanut butter, it's a tale worth telling."

"Good point." We headed down into the sunken in sitting area where I'd smelled the flax seed on the carpet. I knelt down by the end table and put my nose closer to the carpet. I realized it was not the most ladylike position, especially with Detective Briggs standing nearby watching me, but there was no other way.

I sniffed around. The industrial vacuum cleaner had left every trace of odor, including its own metallic motor scent on the carpet. But as I moved my face a bit closer, I picked up a trace of the flax seed smell. "Here, cut these fibers." I pointed to the spot.

Briggs joined me on the floor.

He took out his gloves and the sterile scissors and carefully removed several fibers. He held them up for me to take one more sniff.

"Yep. Dead fish dipped in old paint."

He lowered the fibers into the bag. "Hopefully, they'll track down Celeste soon. I'll need her shoes for evidence." Briggs glanced down at the rug. "Hold on." He lowered his face and grabbed some tweezers out of his pocket. I watched as he tweezed something out of the carpet fibers. He put the nearly microscopic particle in another bag and held it up to the light.

"A flax seed?"

"Looks that way."

"So this was a win-win?" I asked.

"Looks that way." He pushed to his feet and then gallantly offered me his hand. Which I took. His grip was warm and strong and confident. Just what I expected.

I got to my feet and brushed off the carpet lint. "Where to next?"

"Back to town. Maybe by then, I'll have gotten word from highway patrol. Celeste couldn't have gotten too far."

Mr. Trumble was just finishing his angry lecture to the maintenance man as we walked past. He joined us at Briggs' request.

"Mr. Trumble, I'll probably be taking official statements from some of your staff this week, including you. I just wanted to give you a heads up."

"Of course. Whatever you need. Did you find out who killed Ms. Fitch?"

"Possibly. But don't let Mr. Hermann know anything yet. I need to confirm some things first. Then I'll speak to him."

"Naturally. That was fast. Only four days," Mr. Trumble said as he pushed the button on the elevator.

"Really?" Briggs sighed. "Felt like an eternity to me."

* * *

As I sat down in the passenger seat of the car, a voice came through the fuzzy sounding speaker on the dash. I wasn't well versed in official police speak, but it sounded as if they'd stopped Celeste before she'd gotten on the highway.

Briggs climbed into the driver's seat and picked up the radio. The officer on the other end repeated what he'd said. Briggs replied with 'Roger. Over and out'.

"They stopped her just a few miles from here. I hate to drag you along on an arrest, but if I head back to town first—"

"Are you kidding? Drag me along, please."

Briggs started the car and we pulled out onto the road. "As you've probably noticed, Miss Pinkerton, I'm not a big user of technology. I still prefer to keep my notes on paper."

"I might have noticed that." I'd leave out the part where I decided it was cute that he used pen and paper instead of a tablet. "Aside from basics on a computer and my cell phone, I'm not a technology user either."

"Then maybe you won't know the answer to this question. Is it possible to set a different ringtone for different callers? Say a certain song when it's someone you know well?"

I faced him. "Do you mean like a Tom Petty song when it's your sister, who also adores Tom Petty? Yes, that's entirely possible. I can't believe that didn't occur to me before."

"Nor me. I guess we are both a couple of old timers. Tom Petty is still cool to us and technological devices don't interest us."

"I suppose if we're going to work on these cases together," I continued on right past his amused grin. "Then one of us should learn more about technology."

All traces of the storm had passed and the sky was bright. Briggs pulled his sunglasses off the visor and put them on. "I don't know. It seems as long as we have that remarkable nose of yours with us, we'll do fine without the tech knowledge."

I knew my smile was ridiculously big, but I didn't care.

"The truth is, Miss Pinkerton, it would have taken a lot longer to solve this case if not for you and your hypero—" He looked at me for assistance.

"Hyperosmia. And thank you. Glad to lend my nose anytime." We passed a sign pointing to the Mayfield Cemetery, which reminded me of my trip to the Hawksworth family plot. "Detective Briggs, I visited the Graystone Church graveyard because that's one of the odd things I do in my spare time. I noticed there was an unmarked grave in the Hawksworth family plot. Do you know who is buried there?"

"There are several theories on that. None of them proven. You'd have to dig deeper to find the truth. I'm sure it's somewhere in the town records and newspaper stories. One theory is that Mrs. Hawksworth had a baby who died at birth. Another more scandalous explanation is that Bertram Hawksworth fathered an illegitimate baby with another woman and the baby died at birth. Choose your ending, I suppose."

"Was that grave filled before the family was murdered?"

"As far as I know. Hawksworth had purchased the plot for his family years earlier, but I'm sure he didn't expect them to fill it all at once. And obviously he was too important of man to be asked point blank about the unmarked grave."

I rubbed my chin. "Interesting."

He turned toward the highway on ramp. There were several police cars stopped along the side of the road behind and in front of a light blue van. I could see a fretful looking Celeste pacing alongside one of the squad cars, looking thoroughly angry and petrified all at once.

Detective Briggs parked his car behind the last squad car and got out. He talked to several of the officers before walking over to Celeste. I stepped out of the car but hung back, not wanting to tread on official police business. But I kept an ear turned that direction.

"I would like to know just what this is about," Celeste snapped. But there was a waver in her voice that couldn't be missed.

"Miss Bower, I'm going to start with something easy. How many sisters do you have?" Briggs asked.

"One. Why do you ask? Did something—"

"Your sister is fine. I just need you to text her and ask her to call you."

The traffic and the voices of the other policemen were drowning out too much of the conversation. It was my nose that had gotten us to this point. I decided I could move my talented smeller closer to the action.

Celeste pulled out her phone. It was easy to see that her fingers were trembling as she texted her sister.

"I demand to know why I'm doing this," she said.

"Two reasons," Briggs said in his usual relaxed tone. "I'll tell you the second one first. You'll need to talk to a family member to let them know that you are going to be delayed in Mayfield."

"What?" She glanced around at all the faces and sneered my direction just as her phone rang. It was Tom Petty's song Free Fallin'.

"That's the second reason I needed you to call your sister. Now answer it and let her know you won't be home today."

Celeste turned her face away and had a quiet, anxious conversation with her sister. She was close to tears by the time she hung up.

"Miss Bower, I need you to pull all your shoes out of the van."

"My shoes? This is getting crazy. I need to call my lawyer." Her face shifted from red to white to red again, all in a matter of seconds. It was hard not to feel some sympathy for the woman.

"My chickens," she said weakly, as it seemed to dawn on her that she had been caught.

Briggs turned to one of the officers. "Officer West, don't you have a farm out on Dawson Grove? Could you make sure Miss Bower's chickens are well cared for until her family can pick them up?"

"Of course, Detective Briggs."

Briggs followed Celeste to the back door of the van. The chickens clucked as Briggs helped her pull a large suitcase to the back. She opened it.

Moments later, Briggs walked over to me with three pairs of shoes, ankle boots, sandals and the running shoes he'd had Celeste slip off. "Do you mind, Miss Pinkerton?"

"Not at all." I sniffed each pair. "Both the sandals and the ankle boots have the flax seed smell."

He passed the shoes off to be marked as evidence and gave Celeste back her running shoes to put on.

Briggs waved over the female police officer to help before turning around to face his suspect.

"I wouldn't have even thought of it if Fitch hadn't made such a scene about being too close to my chickens and Twyla's peanut butter balls," she said quickly. "The old witch had it coming."

"Celeste Bower, you are under arrest for the murder of Marian Fitch."

"She ruined my chances. She destroyed my career," Celeste cried as the officer took over for Briggs.

"I'll get you back to Port Danby, Miss Pinkerton. There might even be time for you to sell flowers today," Briggs said with a smile.

"In between solving major crimes?"

"Yes." Another smile. Two in a row from Briggs was quite an accomplishment on my part. "Well done, Miss Pinkerton."

"Well done, Detective Briggs."

We climbed back into his car to return to Port Danby.

"Oh gosh, I just remembered my bird is loose in town. I hope he hasn't been terrorizing people. He's going to be angry at me for the rest of the day."

"And just what does that entail? How does a crow act when he's angry?"

"He'll sit on his perch and look the other way if I glance his direction. It's basically crow cold shoulder."

Briggs laughed. I could tell that having the weight of this case off his shoulders had taken some stress off of him. I was glad to see it and thought his lighter mood was a good opportunity to remind him about my Thanksgiving feast. The list had grown. Lester would be joining us as well. It seemed his firehouse friends had decided to deep fry a turkey this year and Lester hated to buck tradition. He wanted his turkey 'stuffed and roasted' like a turkey was supposed to be.

"Detective Briggs, my invitation for Thanksgiving still stands. And you don't need to bring a thing. Elsie and I will take care of everything. That is, unless you've made other plans in the meantime."

I realized I knew very little about his personal life other than he rode a motorcycle, he was once married for a brief time and he disliked my neighbor Dash.

He paused.

"That's all right, Detective Briggs. I'm sure you have family or other significant people to spend time with." I was so silly. It was entirely possible he had a steady girlfriend over in Chesterton.

Although if he did, he certainly didn't bring her up much in conversation. Maybe she wasn't all that exciting to talk about, I decided quickly.

"Actually, my family is several states away. I have to work the next day, so I can't fly out to see them. It's been a few years since I had a good Thanksgiving feast. I'll be there."

"Great." I settled back against the seat with a satisfied smile. "All in all, a successful day."

CHAPTER 36

I didn't have quite enough table for five people so Lester brought his fold out card table. We covered it with one of Elsie's white linen table cloths. Lola brought some of her mom's best dishes, and I added my sample centerpieces to the table. They weren't really meant to sit on the same table together, but they looked just fine. And with Elsie's help in the kitchen, the house was bursting with delicious aromas. I had to control my sense of smell just to avoid falling into a dizzy spell from it all.

Nevermore hadn't left the kitchen all afternoon. Lola and I watched in amusement as the cat paced in front of the oven with his tail straight up in the air.

I took a sip of hot cider. "I think he's waiting for *his* bird to come out of the roasting pan."

"I can't blame him." Lola pressed her arm against her stomach. "I'm trying not to snack on those chips and veggies Elsie laid out. I'm saving room for the real food."

Elsie walked in from the living room. "The game has started, so we've lost Lester for awhile." Elsie ladled herself some spiced cider from the pot. "So do you think he's still coming?"

Lola straightened. "Who, Ryder?" she asked enthusiastically.

I tilted my head at her. "Why would my new employee, who doesn't even start until Monday, come to our Thanksgiving feast?" Lola was just a little too excited about my new assistant. I hoped it wasn't going to be a problem. Ryder had been so perfect for the position. It was almost as if he'd walked out of my help wanted advertisement.

"Who is Ryder?" Elsie asked.

"You haven't heard?" Lola waved her hand. "That's right. You've been swamped with holiday pie orders. You missed all kinds of good stuff while you were elbow deep in pie crust dough. Pink hired a new assistant." She sighed dreamily.

Elsie crooked a brow my direction. I nodded to assure her that, yes, Lola had already set her sights on my new assistant.

"He was really too perfect to pass up," I said. Lola agreed readily. "I mean he's very qualified. He just moved back to Chesterton, his home town, after earning a horticulture degree with a minor in fine arts."

"And he's a musician in a band, and he has dark brown hair and blue eyes," Lola added unnecessarily.

"Yes," I quipped. "Those attributes were listed on my help wanted ad as well."

Elsie picked up a carrot stick and dipped it into the dressing. "He seems perfect. Not to sound harsh but why is a new college grad working in a flower shop?"

"He said he wants to earn money to eventually travel the world and study plants. So he's going to live at home and save."

"I'd love to travel the world," Lola said.

Elsie and I both looked at her. Elsie pointed out the obvious first. "Your parents invite you along on their adventures all the time, and you refuse to go."

"Yes, of course. I don't want to travel with them. But Ryder—now that would be different."

Elsie handed her a dipped carrot stick. "Here, eat something. Low blood sugar is making you silly."

The doorbell rang. Suddenly I was in silly mode too. My stomach did a strange little flippity-do. I smoothed my hair back.

"Maybe you should pinch your cheeks for some color," Elsie noted.

I lifted my hands and then realized she was teasing. I pulled off my apron and tossed it at her, before walking to the door.

Detective Briggs looked fine in his official attire, but he sure cleaned up nice when he dressed down. He had on a black sweater that accentuated his impressive physique.

He held out a bottle of wine. "I can't cook my way out of a can of soup, so I decided to play it safe."

I took the wine. "Wonderful. Thank you. Come inside, Detective Briggs. We've got some hot cider heating on the stove."

He walked into the house. "Since we're not on official business, I think it would be all right if you call me James."

I smiled. "And you can call me, Lacey."

"Thanks for having me, Lacey."

"Thank you for coming, James." Hmm, I liked the way it sounded on my lips.

AUTHOR'S NOTE

Sadly, Tom Petty died as this book was in final edits. When I hear a Tom Petty song on the radio, my hand instinctively reaches for the volume knob. He will always be one of my favorite singers. Godspeed, Tom Petty.

Port Danby is preparing for the annual Harbor Holiday Lights Flotilla, and Lacey 'Pink' Pinkerton is anxious to see the colorful boats light up Pickford Beach. But the festive spirits of the town are dampened when one of the boat owners is strangled to death. Lacey enthusiastically volunteers to help Detective Briggs *sniff* out the clues and track down the killer. Once again, she finds herself *nose* deep in a murder mystery.

Mistletoe and Mayhem (Port Danby Cozy Mystery #3) coming November 12th, 2017.

CHERRY, CHOCOLATE AND
PISTACHIO BISCOTTI

View online at: www.londonlovett.com/recipe-box/

Cherry, Chocolate and Pistachio
BISCOTTI

Ingredients:

1/2 cup butter, softened
3/4 cup granulated sugar
2 eggs
2 tsp vanilla
2 cups all-purpose flour

1/12 tsp baking powder
1/4 tsp salt
1 cup roasted, chopped pistachios
3/4 cup mini chocolate chips
3/4 cup dried cherries, chopped

Directions:

1. Preheat over to 350°

2. Chop the roasted pistachios—if they aren't already chopped—and set aside.

3. Chop the dried cherries and set aside.

4. In a medium bowl, mix together flour, baking powder and salt. Set side.

5. In a large bowl, cream together sugar and butter. Mix in eggs and vanilla until well blended.

6. Add dry ingredients into the large bowl and stir until just combined.

7. Stir in chopped pistachios, dried cherries and chocolate chips. Mix until they are well distributed throughout the dough.

8. Grease and flour 2 baking sheets (You can also use baking spray.)

9. Divide dough in half and shape each half into an oblong, flat log.

10. Bake for 26 minutes, until light brown.

11. Remove pan(s) from the oven and allow the logs to cool for 10 minutes.

12. Cut each log into 1 inch slices and turn each slice on its side.

13. Bake the slices for 10 more minutes.

14. Remove from oven, let cool and enjoy!

ABOUT THE AUTHOR

London Lovett is the author of the new Port Danby Cozy Mystery series. She loves getting caught up in a good mystery and baking delicious new treats!

Subscribe to London's newsletter on her site to never miss an update.

https://www.londonlovett.com/
londonlovettwrites@gmail.com

Made in the USA
Las Vegas, NV
14 February 2023